Jessica's heart pounded wildly. What would the criminals do if they knew she was awake, watching them rummage through her backpack? If she moved one inch, her life could be over in an instant. *Go away*, she willed silently, *please just go away*. She practically stopped breathing in an attempt to be completely still. *Please don't kill us.*

Just then, Heather stirred.

"What time is it?" she asked sleepily. Jessica's stomach turned over at the sound of Heather's voice.

Finally, after what seemed like a lifetime, Heather caught sight of the convicts. Instantly, her eyes went wide and her mouth flew open into a scream loud enough to wake the dead. Jessica squeezed her eyes shut. What would happen to them now?

"You're gonna wish you hadn't done that, little lady," a deep, menacing voice said in the dark.

NIGHTMARE IN DEATH VALLEY

Written by
Kate William

Created by
FRANCINE PASCAL

BANTAM BOOKS
NEW YORK · TORONTO · LONDON · SYDNEY · AUCKLAND

RL 6, age 12 and up

NIGHTMARE IN DEATH VALLEY

A Bantam Book / June 1995

Sweet Valley High® is a registered trademark of Francine Pascal
Conceived by Francine Pascal
Produced by Daniel Weiss Associates, Inc.
33 West 17th Street
New York, NY 10011
Cover art by Bruce Emmett

ISBN: 0-553-56634-2

Published simultaneously in the United States and Canada

Bantam Books are published by Bantam Books, a division of Bantam
Doubleday Dell Publishing Group, Inc. Its trademark, consisting of the
words "Bantam Books" and the portrayal of a rooster, is Registered in
U.S. Patent and Trademark Office and in other countries. Marca
Registrada. Bantam Books, 1540 Broadway, New York, New York 10036.

PRINTED IN THE UNITED STATES OF AMERICA

OPM   0 9 8 7 6 5 4 3 2 1

To Mia Pascal Johansson

Chapter 1

"I wish I'd never come on this stupid camping trip," Heather Mallone complained to Elizabeth Wakefield. Her words were almost drowned out in the pouring rain. A sudden thunder shower was drenching Death Valley.

Elizabeth shielded her eyes from raindrops the size of hailstones. She spotted a rock overhang nearby that they could stand under for shelter. "We can't help that now," she said to Heather. "Let's head for that dry spot."

Heather began to scramble toward the shelter, but after two steps she cried out in pain. "Ow! My ankle!" she howled, falling into a shallow pool of water.

Elizabeth pushed her wet hair out of her face to see Heather sloshing and splashing in a frantic effort to stand. "Give me your hand," Elizabeth yelled over the deafening noise of the rain. She bent down to pull Heather up. "I'll help you."

1

Hanging on to Elizabeth's arm, Heather began to limp toward the overhang.

With her free hand Elizabeth managed to signal her boyfriend, Todd Wilkins, and point in the direction of the shelter. Wearily, Todd responded with a thumbs-up sign and called to Bruce Patman, Ken Matthews, and Jessica Wakefield, Elizabeth's twin sister, to follow him.

As she helped Heather negotiate the slippery rocks, Elizabeth wondered how they'd got themselves into this situation.

The six of them had been chosen, as the top student leaders of Sweet Valley High, to participate in a four-day desert-survival hike. The Sweet Valley Survival School had sponsored the special trip to promote the expansion of its successful course on leadership training. The school administrators had selected the group based on their special individual accomplishments, such as Todd's position as key player on the basketball team, and Ken's star achievement in football. Because Heather and Jessica were cocaptains of the cheerleading squad, they had been chosen, too.

Their survival-school trainers, Kay Jansen and Brad Mainzer, had taught them map and compass reading, camping, and mountaineering, as well as basic survival skills. Then, on Monday morning, Kay and Brad had driven the SVH group to the starting point for their desert camping trip. Elizabeth, Ken, Todd, Jessica, Bruce, and Heather had thanked their trainers and hoisted their packs over their shoulders.

Just before they'd hiked off into the desert, Kay had warned them that they had to reach their final goal, Desert Oasis, in four days, or risk getting caught in a serious desert rainstorm!

They'd been making good progress—until Tuesday afternoon, when Elizabeth had found a satchel of gold deep in a desert mine shaft. Next to the satchel lay a treasure map marked with a series of black X's, indicating caves where more treasure was hidden. The group ended up abandoning their original course to search for the gold.

If all that wasn't bad enough, Elizabeth now thought glumly, they had made room in their packs for each bag of treasure by foolishly tossing out most of their food. Minutes ago they had arrived at the treasure map's final X—only to find a cave harboring six skeletons and a bag of scorpions! Horrified, the group had raced quickly out of the cave just when a clap of thunder had crashed from the sky and thick drops of rain pelted down.

Now it was Thursday night at seven P.M., exactly when they were supposed to be meeting the bus at Desert Oasis. But instead they were miles from their destination, drenched to the skin in the driving storm, with a dangerously low supply of food.

And to top it all off, Heather had sprained her ankle that afternoon, and it had swollen to three times its normal size. She could barely make it to the shelter, much less climb down the slippery mesa.

Exhausted, Elizabeth nevertheless bravely steered Heather over the slick, rocky terrain.

Suddenly a two-foot-long scaly Gila monster ran across their path.

"What is that horrible thing?" Heather screamed. She broke into miserable sobs. Elizabeth grimly led her to the overhang. *Things can't possibly get any worse than this,* she thought.

The others were already under the shelter, throwing down their packs and wringing out their T-shirts. Heather sniffled loudly as she eased herself onto the hard ground.

"The mascara running all over your face is a nice improvement, Heather," Jessica offered, squeezing the water out of her long blond hair.

"You don't look too wonderful yourself," Heather retorted.

"Oh, I think the wet-dog look really suits you, Wakefield," Bruce said.

"How about the drowned-rat look, which you've perfected, Patman?" Jessica shot back from under a handful of hair. She stood up, glaring at Bruce, then shivered suddenly. "Fifteen minutes ago I was roasting, now I'm freezing," she complained, vigorously rubbing her arms.

"If Your Highness wishes, I'll call the weather bureau and request a change," Todd said.

"Don't get grouchy with me, Wilkins," Jessica said in a warning tone, pulling a blue flannel shirt out of her pack.

Elizabeth noticed that Heather was shivering too. Yesterday she had fallen into a raging river, and the rest of the group had barely managed to pull her out

4

before she drowned. Her sleeping bag had floated to the surface—but, unfortunately, her backpack had been lost.

"Heather, would you like to borrow a flannel shirt?" Elizabeth offered, unzipping her backpack.

Rubbing the running mascara off her face, Heather nodded, and Elizabeth handed her a red plaid shirt. "Not quite the Christian Dior sweater I lost in the river, but it'll do—thanks," Heather said breezily as she pulled the warm shirt on. "I can't believe I lost my brush and my entire makeup kit. I don't even want to know what my hair must look like."

"Well, if you wear a sleeping-bag case over your head for the rest of the trip, you won't make the rest of us too sick," Jessica said, glaring at Heather.

"Jessica, she lost her backpack—have a little patience and compassion," Todd pleaded. Then he added dryly, "I'll find you a dictionary so you can look those words up."

Elizabeth glanced from her sister to her boyfriend. Everyone's nerves were about to shatter. They'd all barely spoken to each other all day, but silence had been better than this pointless bickering. Elizabeth realized that now more than ever the group would have to find a way to work together again—or they'd never get out of the desert alive.

"Todd, how about helping me get a fire started?" Elizabeth suggested. But Todd was still glaring at Jessica.

"Jessica," Todd continued coldly, ignoring Elizabeth, "you know, we wouldn't even be in this mess if it weren't for your navigating us toward the last spot on the treasure map instead of toward Desert Oasis. If we never get out of this, it's all your fault."

"Is that right? Well, for your information, *Todd,* at least I can read a map—*some* people, I'm sure, were too busy thinking about *basketball* to have paid attention during training," Jessica said, rolling up the sleeves of her flannel shirt. "And besides, it's Bruce's fault for even going into a mine shaft in the first place. Kay and Brad *warned* us to stay out of them."

Instead of answering Jessica, Bruce turned his cold gaze toward Elizabeth. "Elizabeth was the one who found the map. If it weren't for her, we'd—"

"Drop it," Ken said, tossing a rock into the canyon in disgust. "Would everyone just shut up and face the fact that we're stuck in this totally dismal place? And there's no obvious way out."

The group fell silent. Elizabeth thought back to the start of the trip on Monday. It seemed like a thousand years ago. She'd been convinced that she really had what it took to excel in a survival course. But she'd been wrong. She knew the whole disastrous situation was as much her fault as anybody's. Her greed, both for the gold and for the story she wanted to write about it, had gotten her where she was now. Elizabeth had a lot of respect for Kay Jansen, and Kay had believed in her. Elizabeth felt as if she'd let everyone down.

"Hey, look," Ken called out, running to the edge of the shelter. "The rain stopped."

"The desert is totally unpredictable," Todd said.

"A tornado will probably come along in a few minutes," Bruce said.

"Well, what are we standing around for?" Jessica asked impatiently. "Let's get out of here before we get hit with a tidal wave—or something worse! Maybe we can still catch the bus." She slung her backpack over her shoulders and began tromping back to the trail.

"Catch the bus?" Heather called after her, trying to push herself up from the ground. "You're the original dumb blonde, aren't you, Jessica?"

Jessica spun around and took two giant steps back toward Heather. "That does it, Mallone, that was the last straw," she said through clenched teeth.

"She has a point, Jessica," Bruce said, raising his eyebrows. "Though I never thought of it in such colorful terms."

"Hey, hey, hey!" Elizabeth shouted to the group. "Let's not start fighting again. OK?" She turned to her sister. "Jess, they're right. The bus has left without us by now."

Jessica planted her hands on her hips. "So what do you plan to do, homestead in the desert? No, thanks."

"And what do *you* plan to do?" Todd inquired with irritation. "Hitchhike to the nearest coffee shop?"

Elizabeth sighed and looked out from under the shelter as Todd and Jessica continued to bicker. *How are we ever going to get home?* she thought with despair.

"It'll be dark soon," Elizabeth finally said. "Looks like this is home for the night. Let's get some sleep."

"Fine with me," Jessica said, yanking her sleeping bag from its case and spreading it out in the middle of the shelter floor.

"There isn't enough room for all of us to lay out our bags under this shelter," Elizabeth pointed out. She stood up and pulled on her backpack. "Come on. We'll have to sleep in the cave."

"You expect me to spend the night with six skeletons and a hundred scorpions?" Jessica demanded through chattering teeth. She was standing at the edge of the cave, shivering. Her wet shorts were sticking to her legs. She felt as if she needed about twenty-five more flannel shirts before she would even begin to feel warm.

"Save a scorpion for me—I like them for breakfast," Bruce said dryly, tossing his stuff onto the cave floor. "With toast and eggs."

"You're a sick boy, Bruce," Jessica responded. Being stuck for one more night with Bruce and Heather and Todd was bad enough. But now Jessica was supposed to sleep in this haunted cave in the middle of nowhere. She'd much rather be home, taking a luxurious forest-scented bubble bath, and getting ready to go to sleep on satin sheets in her own bed.

Jessica watched Elizabeth neatly lay out her bag, then march around like some kind of drill sergeant, making sure everyone else's sleeping bags had been

8

laid out to dry. Her twin sister was taking this whole camping trip so seriously—the way she did everything.

Although they'd been born only four minutes apart and looked identical on the outside, inside they couldn't have been more different. The twins had the same soft blond hair, eyes the color of the Pacific Ocean, and delicate features—but that's where the similarities ended. Jessica would much rather be *in* the Pacific Ocean right now, wearing a new bikini just purchased on a shopping spree at Lisette's. Elizabeth, on the other hand, was obviously thriving on the challenge and responsibility of this horrible trip!

Even the twins' favorite activities at home were totally opposite: Jessica was a star cheerleader, and Elizabeth spent her free time working for the school newspaper, *The Oracle*. Although they were both popular in school, Jessica's best friend, rich and flashy Lila Fowler, had absolutely nothing in common with Elizabeth's best friend, straight-A student Enid Rollins, whom Jessica considered to be sort of a nerd.

Well, Elizabeth might think we should stay in this soggy cave with a pile of dried corpses, she thought. *But I have other plans.*

"You guys, sleeping here is demented. This place is probably cursed. I say we take off now," Jessica declared.

"Oh, give it a rest, Jess," Ken said, snapping a dry twig in his fingers. "Do you think any of us love the idea of a slumber party in a cemetery? But we're in this together—it won't kill you to cooperate."

"And it won't kill you to be nice to me. We're supposed to like each other, or had you forgotten?" Jessica snarled.

Ken came up behind Jessica and gave her shoulders a gentle squeeze. He kissed her lightly on the neck. She turned around and looked up into his handsome face. Then she closed her eyes and raised her lips to his. But he only kissed her quickly on her forehead and walked off. A few feet away he knelt on the cave floor and started making a fire.

Bruce slumped down on the ground into a cross-legged position. He held his hands toward the leaping flames. "Whoever's serving hot chocolate, don't forget the whipped cream on mine," he said dully.

"Keep dreaming, Bruce," Todd responded as he, Elizabeth, and Heather sat against the cave wall and stretched their feet toward the warmth of the fire.

Jessica was still standing, staring at her boyfriend. At least he'd *been* her boyfriend before this nightmare camping trip; she wasn't so sure anymore. Ken was hardly paying attention to her. Besides, she might never be able to forgive him for snubbing her by placing Heather next to him when they'd had to make a human chain to cross that dangerous river. And then he'd blamed Jessica when stupid Heather had panicked and fallen into the rapids! Well, it wasn't Jessica's fault. None of what happened to them in Death Valley had been her fault.

And now, as if Heather hadn't hogged enough attention, the Bride of Frankenstein had a sprained

10

ankle the size of a football, which she'd twisted while trying to leap across a boulder field.

"I don't know about staying the whole night here, either," Heather said. "At least the skeletons are dead. Real, live escaped convicts could be headed toward us right this moment."

Jessica rolled her eyes. Heather couldn't shut up for five minutes about the escaped convicts. When Heather had pulled out her little portable TV on Tuesday to watch her soap opera, they'd seen a news flash about three convicts who'd escaped from a prison not far from Death Valley. Heather was immediately convinced that the convicts were hot on their trail. Just that morning she had come trotting breathlessly up to the group with some story about having seen three men in blue jumpsuits brewing coffee at a campsite. Of course, they *had* to be the escaped convicts.

"She could be right," Ken said, looking around the group and then gazing with sympathy at Heather. Jessica shot a fierce look at Heather.

"I know I'm right," Heather said, stumbling to her feet. "I've just got this creepy feeling."

"I bet they want those skeletons. They're a great collector's item," Bruce said sarcastically.

"I bet they want the gold," Heather snapped. "And by the way," she added coolly, "you can stop making fun of me anytime." She started to pivot but stopped in mid turn. Her knees seemed to buckle as she let out a gasp of pain. Shadows leaped across the cave walls as Ken stood quickly and caught

11

Heather by the arm, barely breaking her fall.

"Relax and rest your foot," Ken said gently to Heather. Jessica felt daggers of jealousy in the pit of her stomach. *That girl never quits!*

"Can't we all just leave?" Heather pleaded as Ken made her comfortable. "I can walk, I really can." Ken was probably sorry he didn't bring a nice pillow to fluff up for her, Jessica noted bitterly.

"I don't think we should try to leave tonight," Elizabeth said in an even voice, shaking her head. "The chances of our falling and breaking our necks in the dark are probably much higher than the chances of being assaulted by convicts."

Jessica glanced at the pile of skeletons. A lone scorpion crawled along the back of the cave. "Well, how can you be so sure?" she demanded.

Elizabeth raised an eyebrow at Jessica. "A minute ago you were scoffing at the idea of convicts running loose nearby," Elizabeth observed.

"So what? The whole point is that if two us have the creeps, then let's get out of here," Jessica said, still standing, with her hands on her hips.

"I'm not going anywhere," Bruce said, leaning back on his sleeping bag and lazily crossing his hands behind his head. "I'm going to lie here and pretend I'm floating on an air mattress in my swimming pool."

"Count me out, too," Todd said.

"I have to go along with staying put," Ken said with a shrug.

Elizabeth threw up her hands and stared first at Heather, then at Jessica. "Look," Elizabeth said, "you guys are welcome to try to make your way in the dark, but you'll have to do it alone. The rest of us plan to stay right here until sunrise."

"Heather may not be able to move too fast," Todd pointed out. "You might have to carry her part of the way."

Great group of friends, Jessica thought. *They really stand by you when the chips are down.* She looked over at Heather with open disgust. The idea of carrying her archenemy down the trail was about as appealing as eating spiders.

"Fine," Jessica huffed. "Have it your way."

"Where are you going now?" Elizabeth asked Jessica wearily as she watched her sister drag her sleeping bag out of the cave. Elizabeth felt a chill as the air touched her with cold fingers.

"Oh, I just have this urge to commune with the stars," Jessica answered testily. Elizabeth sighed. Jessica was obviously mad that everyone else voted down her plan to hike off the mesa, so she was storming off to sleep by herself. Elizabeth followed her sister to the cave's edge.

"Jessica, it could start raining again," Elizabeth pointed out, wrapping her arms around her torso to stay warm.

"I'll be fine," Jessica sniffed. "Tell room service not to wake me in the morning. I plan to sleep in."

"Come on back with the rest of us." Elizabeth tried to sound patient, but she was exhausted almost to the point of tears. *I can't give in to desperation,*

13

she told herself. *One of us has to stay strong or we'll never make it.*

"Why? Are we going to make popcorn and watch old movies?" Jessica said with as much sarcasm as she could muster. Then she shivered again. Elizabeth saw that even the flannel shirt wasn't enough to keep Jessica warm in the cold desert night.

"Hold that thought," Elizabeth said lightly. "That's the first thing we'll do when we get home, even if we walk in the door at two in the afternoon." She walked back into the cave and rummaged in her pack, fishing out a Sweet Valley High football sweatshirt. Maybe seeing the logo from back home would give her sister some perspective. She brought the sweatshirt to Jessica.

"What's that for?" Jessica asked, glancing up but refusing to look directly at Elizabeth.

"You looked cold," her twin answered. "I thought you might need something warm to wear."

"I've got something warm to wear," Jessica answered stiffly. "I don't need any of your clothes." She turned her back on Elizabeth and stalked off. It was as if Jessica had slammed a door between them.

Usually, Jessica rummaged through Elizabeth's closet without asking, borrowing all of her new outfits before the tags had even been removed. Although Elizabeth complained about it, she knew that sharing clothes had always been part of the easy bond between the twins. But now Jessica wouldn't even accept a cotton sweatshirt as a peace offering!

"Hey, don't shove my sleeping bag over there!

Now it's right on top of a rock," Elizabeth heard Bruce say behind her. She turned away from Jessica and went back inside the cave.

"I didn't touch your sleeping bag, so back off," Todd said sharply.

"Look, we're all too tired for this," Elizabeth said, pulling on the sweatshirt that Jessica had refused. Todd shot her an irritated look. Bruce opened his mouth to say something but then waved his hand in disgust. He took long steps out of the cave and settled down to sit on a rock.

"I don't feel safe here at all. I'd still much rather hike out tonight," Heather announced, arranging her long blond hair on her shoulders. "The only way I can stay in this cave all night is if I can sleep between the guys."

Bruce was ignoring everyone and didn't respond. "Sure," Ken said. He looked at Todd, who shrugged in agreement.

"It's fine with me," Todd said in the nicest tone of voice Elizabeth had heard from him all day. Then she remembered how he had gently bandaged Heather's sprained ankle. She felt an uncomfortable tightness in her chest.

Suddenly Jessica stuck her head into the cave. She tossed her hair and made an attempt at one of her charming smiles—though it came off more like a grimace.

"So what are we up to in here?" she asked casually, as if she happened to be strolling by. Elizabeth knew Jessica had overheard every word of the conversation.

"Heather's still kind of freaked, so she's going to sleep between Ken and me," Todd explained, throwing a quick grin to Heather.

Elizabeth wanted to scream. A few hours ago she'd been able to commiserate with her sister about Heather. How could that understanding between them have vanished so suddenly? As twins, they'd always been able to communicate without words. *Jessica, please look at me,* she silently begged.

Jessica gazed for a single second into Elizabeth's eyes. The look was pure ice.

Chapter 2

"Is anyone especially fond of sleeping on scorpions, or can we at least sweep them out of the cave?" Jessica inquired, standing with her arms crossed over her chest.

"What do you care?" Todd said, glancing at the cave's entrance. "Aren't you setting up shop outside?"

"Nope, just shaking my bag out. I've decided to join the party in the House of the Dead," Jessica answered. *Heather's going to have Ken to herself all night over my dead body!* she thought.

"Well, I can't seem to find the vacuum cleaner, but how's this for a broom?" Ken said, holding up a bunch of sagebrush.

Jessica, Elizabeth, Todd, and Bruce picked their sleeping bags up off the cave floor and dumped them outside the entrance. Then they all pulled up their own bunches of sagebrush. Jessica could barely stand to clean up her room at home, much less do a disgusting job like sweeping scorpions out of a cave. But extreme circumstances called for extreme measures.

"Heather, here. You can use some of my sagebrush," Elizabeth said, pulling her bunch apart.

"I don't think I can do this, you guys," Heather said, looking pained. "Every time I try to bend down, my ankle absolutely kills."

Jessica snorted in disgust. *Typical.* She wondered if she could strangle Heather without anyone noticing. The winner of the coveted Miss Black Widow award appeared to have this bunch of mush-for-brains guys wrapped around her little finger—but even they wouldn't let her get away with this kind of nonsense!

"No problem, Heather, you just hang out and let us take care of it," Ken said generously.

Jessica practically shredded her sagebrush. So the bitter truth was out: Ken was a total sap. So what? Plenty of guys would beg for a date with her. She would find herself a boyfriend with some spine!

"I don't see any more scorpions," Elizabeth finally said with a sigh. "I think they're all swept out."

"Good riddance. They'll make nice cactus fertilizer," Bruce said. He tossed his sagebrush out the cave entrance.

"Well, let's get the bags arranged," Heather said in a tired voice, which barely masked her enthusiasm for the upcoming "arrangement." Heather threw Jessica an unmistakable look of satisfaction. *She may think she's won,* Jessica thought, *but she's dead wrong if she thinks she can count me out permanently!*

18

Jessica dragged her bag in from outside and threw it down in a corner of the cave.

"You might want to reconsider where you lay your bedding, Miss Wakefield," Bruce said with an English accent in a sinister, suggestive tone.

Jessica followed Bruce's gaze to the cave ceiling a few feet above where she planned to sleep. She caught her breath at the sight of several ominous, knifelike limestone stalactites. She heard Bruce laughing cruelly as she moved the bag a few feet away.

Elizabeth and Bruce tossed their bags at opposite ends of the cave. Then Todd, Ken, and Heather laid theirs in the middle, all snuggled together. Jessica seethed watching them, but she was determined not to show it. She busied herself changing into a long-sleeved striped shirt for bed. She was so tired of wearing the SVSS T-shirts and khaki shorts. *The boring clothes are what's bringing us all this bad luck!* The absolute second she got home she intended to grab Lila and buy out the mall. She deserved at least a dozen new outfits after this fiasco.

Jessica took a drink from her water bottle. It was less than half-full. She'd give anything to be sitting at a booth at the Dairi Burger, chugging down a case of diet cola. And after this endless, hideous day of trudging through the sun, then getting soaked to the bone, she was famished. But how much food did they have left? Suddenly a terrible thought occured to her. *What if I starve to death out here?* Jessica glanced over at the skeletons. *Is that what happened to them?*

19

"Hey, does anybody have anything that could pass for dinner?" Todd called out, digging around in his backpack.

"I don't see anything in my pack but granola bars, and very few of them at that," Elizabeth answered from her end of the cave.

"Same here," Ken and Heather said at the same time, then started laughing like idiots. Jessica felt her heart twist.

"All right, you two. Save your giggling for later," Bruce said, throwing a sideways glance at Jessica. Jessica stared coldly into Bruce's eyes. She'd thought she already knew the worst side of Bruce Patman, but this trip was proving that he was even more horrible than she'd guessed. She blew him a kiss and imagined stealing into his house and tying all his expensive clothes in knots.

"Well, this is it," Elizabeth said, pulling up something from the bottom of her pack. "Two boxes of macaroni and cheese."

"For the six of us?" Todd said in dismay. "I feel like I could eat sixteen of them by myself."

"I have such a craving for a cheeseburger," Heather said dreamily.

"With french fries," Ken added.

Jessica glared at them. She was too annoyed to sit around and listen to them babbling about imaginary food. It was time for somebody to take action.

"Let me have them," Jessica said, taking the macaroni boxes out of Elizabeth's hand. "I volunteer to make dinner."

Elizabeth clutched her heart, as if she were about to faint. "I've never heard you utter those words before, Jessica," Elizabeth gasped.

"Well, enjoy it while it lasts," Jessica snapped. She dumped the boxes of macaroni and dried cheese into the cooking pot, then poured in a cup of water and stirred the mixture impatiently. She usually wasn't a fan of boxed dinners, even when their parents were working late and she and Elizabeth had to fend for themselves. But the aroma of noodles and cheese rising from the steaming pot was better than anything she'd ever smelled in her life.

Jessica spooned the minuscule portions into bowls and passed them around to Elizabeth, Heather, Todd, and Ken, who started eating noisily. Jessica scooped Bruce's macaroni into a bowl and held it out to him.

"Hey, the portions aren't even," Bruce complained loudly, not touching the bowl. "You skimped on mine."

"That's not true," Jessica said. She wanted nothing more than to stuff Bruce into a small space capsule and shoot him permanently into the next galaxy. But that didn't mean she would actually try to *starve* him.

"Yes, it is true," Bruce said, his face darkening.

"Bruce, shut up and eat. Everyone else is about done, anyway," Jessica said. She looked around at everyone licking their bowls. It didn't take long to eat five bites of macaroni.

"Why don't you add a spoonful of yours?" Bruce said menacingly.

"Look, take it or leave it," Jessica finally said. "Does this look like a fancy restaurant?" She half handed and half tossed him his bowl. It grazed his index finger and fell, spilling the meager portion of macaroni onto the dirt.

"That's it, I've had it!" Bruce shouted. He lunged at Jessica.

Todd threw down his empty bowl and jumped up to restrain Bruce.

"Bruce, you're insane!" Jessica yelled.

"Well, you're a conniving—" Bruce began to spit out, breaking free of Todd's grip and charging toward Jessica.

Suddenly Elizabeth was on her feet and standing between Jessica and Bruce.

"Don't you dare touch my sister," Elizabeth hissed, giving Bruce a hard shove backward. Jessica gaped at her twin, shocked. *Mild-mannered Elizabeth!* Jessica placed a hand on Elizabeth's shoulder from behind and felt the tension drain from her sister's body.

Elizabeth wilted slightly and placed a hand on her forehead. "We can't deteriorate into fighting like this," Elizabeth said quietly. "We're facing too much danger. We can't destroy each other and expect to survive." Everyone fell silent for a moment.

Just then they heard a rustling in the brush outside the cave, and Jessica rushed out to see what it was.

22

"What is it?" Heather called in alarm.

"It's just a wild fox," Jessica casually called back. She watched the fox's yellow eyes staring at her in the darkness. A chill ran up her spine.

Jessica cleaned up the few dishes and settled into her bag, wishing she could sleep for about three years. She watched world-champion do-gooder, Todd, help revolting, helpless Heather get into her sleeping bag.

Just as Heather got all snuggled up in her bag, Ken came along and folded up a flannel shirt into a pillow for her. Jessica closed her eyes, telling herself that she couldn't care less what Ken did. But then, as she opened her eyes again and saw Ken nestling into his bag right next to Heather's, Jessica couldn't help feeling a sharp pang of jealousy.

What was Heather so worried about, anyway? A bunch of escaped convicts who were probably in Mexico by now? It was true that Jessica's bag of gold had mysteriously disappeared from her pack, but someone in the group had probably taken it and re-fused to fess up. Jessica still didn't believe Heather had actually seen any escaped prisoners. She was just freaking out to get attention.

But as Jessica drifted off to sleep, she saw an image of the wild fox's cruel yellow eyes. *What if it had been one of the convicts staring at me from the brush? What would I have done then?*

Elizabeth listened to the soft, even breathing in the cave. Everyone but she was asleep. A coyote howled in the distance. Her stomach growled. For a few minutes she'd almost forgotten how hungry she was. She couldn't believe she'd actually gone along with abandoning most of their food supply to make room for gold!

She crawled deeper into her bag and stared at the cave ceiling. Then, she trained the beam of her flashlight into her pack to find the old diary that she'd discovered in the mine shaft at the same time she'd found the gold. She carefully pulled out the fragile book. The entries were dated 1849, the year of the California Gold Rush. She silently read the final entry:

Dear Diary,

I don't know how long we can go on, but I fear for us all. Greed over the gold has torn our group apart. There is much squabbling among us, and all our cooperation has given way to hatred and mistrust. People are not themselves. Even gentle Mary has shocked me with the change that has taken place in her. Today I saw her strike William in anger with a blow so hard as to knock him from his feet. I know how the two of them care for one another. Or did.

We are in great danger. We have barely enough food to see us through another day, and we've no idea how to find our way out of this barren land. We were so filled with hope

24

and adventure when we started our journey
in Oregon. Now all is lost.

The rest of the pages were blank. Elizabeth put away the papers and looked over at the skeletons. She felt a shiver run up her spine.

What happened to them? she wondered. How did they all die? And what's going to happen to us?

Chapter 3

Elizabeth woke very early on Friday morning to a faint scratching sound. She rolled over and saw several small lizards scampering around Jessica's head. Jessica heard them, too, and sprang awake. The twins caught each other's eye. Jessica glanced at one of the lizards and turned down the corners of her mouth in disgust; then she looked over at Todd, Heather, and Ken and stuck out her tongue. Elizabeth covered her mouth to suppress a laugh.

Jessica arched an eyebrow at Elizabeth and picked up one of the lizards by the tail. With a quick flick of her wrist, she flung it at Heather. Heather jerked awake, swatting the air with both hands. She opened her eyes to find herself face-to-face with the lizard, which jumped onto her head, then scampered into a hole in the cave wall.

Heather bolted upright. "Aaaaaahhhh!" she screamed. "Lizards!"

Todd and Ken woke with looks of shock, as if someone had clapped a pair of cymbals right over their heads. Elizabeth glanced at Jessica again, and both sisters pressed their faces into their sleeping bags to stifle their giggles.

"What's your problem?" Bruce groaned to Heather.

"How would you like it if you had lizards running all over you at the crack of dawn?" Heather said in a shrill voice.

"Oh, I much prefer when they choose a reasonable hour, like eight P.M., to go running all over me," Bruce yawned.

"Heather, this is the desert," Ken said, leaning on both elbows with an annoyed look on his face. "What do you expect to see, penguins?" He glanced over at Elizabeth and rolled his eyes.

"I guess the day has begun, ready or not," Todd said, rubbing his face with his hands. "OK, give me one hundred jumping jacks and thirty push-ups."

"Right, Sarge," Jessica said sarcastically, stretching her arms.

Elizabeth rolled up her sleeping bag and walked outside the cave. The sun was beginning to rise in the blue-and-purple sky, and she caught her breath at the beauty of the desert. Even if they never made it out of Death Valley alive, at least for the moment she had the vivid colors of the vast sky in front of her.

"Mmmm, can you smell the lilac?" Ken asked, coming up behind her. She turned and watched him as he gazed at the sunrise. He ran a hand through his hair, which caught the rising light.

28

"I sure can," Elizabeth said, inhaling deeply. "Look at all those orange and yellow desert flowers."

"They must have opened up from the rain yesterday."

"Uh-huh," Elizabeth agreed as they shared the quiet moment.

"Hey, Liz!" Jessica called out to Elizabeth. "Let's hit the trail. We've got another day of hot, endless hiking through snake pits and scrub brush to look forward to."

"We'd better take an inventory of our food supply before we go," Elizabeth suggested as she and Ken walked back into the cave. They laid out on the ground what little food was left among the six of them.

"I've got four granola bars, and that's it," Elizabeth said.

"Three granola bars here," Todd reported. Heather and Ken had one granola bar each.

"Great," Ken finally said. "Nine granola bars. That's only enough for breakfast today, and then two more tiny meals."

"If you call half a granola bar a meal," Jessica said.

"Well, I'm ready for my three square inches of breakfast," Todd said.

"Coming right up," Jessica answered, picking up a package containing two cinnamon granola bars. She tore the wax paper package open with her teeth and broke the bars into four halves. Ken took a chocolate-chip bar out of an already open package and split it with Bruce.

Elizabeth cheerfully accepted her cinnamon half. She tried to stifle thoughts of how they'd be eating two granola bars apiece right now if she hadn't let herself get carried away with dreams of the great story she was going to write about finding the gold. Would this tiny amount of nourishment keep them from starving until they reached Desert Oasis?

Looking around at the group, Elizabeth saw the fatigue on everyone's face. How could they possibly hike all day with so little food in their stomachs? And today was only Friday. What about tomorrow? *Snap out of it, Elizabeth,* she told herself. *All you can do is take it one moment at a time.*

They all stuffed their sleeping bags into their small vinyl sacks and strapped them onto their backpacks. Ken and Jessica finished packing and stood outside surveying the landscape.

"Here, I'll carry the pan from last night in my pack," Todd said to Elizabeth, running a hand over her cheek. She looked into his brown eyes. "We'll be OK," he whispered.

"I hope you're right," she murmured. "Let's get out of here before anything else can happen." His lips brushed hers and he resumed packing his gear. Elizabeth felt a familiar warmth as she watched Todd's muscled arms zip his pack closed. Then she thought back to the fight over food that had taken place the previous night, and she shuddered.

She couldn't believe she'd actually shoved Bruce so hard. At least protecting her twin from Bruce had led to some sort of unspoken truce with Jessica.

Elizabeth picked up her loaded pack and took one last look in the cave to be sure she hadn't forgotten anything. She turned to step outside, but Bruce blocked her way.

"I say we go for it and finish the granola bars," Bruce said in an authoritative, strangely accusing tone. Elizabeth stared at him. Was he serious?

"Bruce, you heard what they said in survival training," Elizabeth responded. "When supplies are low, a little bit each day will sustain you much longer than a whole lot at once and then none later."

"Come on, we'll be back at Desert Oasis in no time. We'll need all the strength we can get for a final push," Bruce argued.

"Bruce, read my lips," Elizabeth said, getting angry. "It's a bad idea. It could take longer than we think to get back." She slung her pack over her shoulders and stepped over a pile of crumbled limestone rocks on her way out.

"How do *you* know how long it'll take to get back? Did you map this region in a past life or something?" Bruce said aggressively, blocking Elizabeth's path.

"Excuse me, would you mind letting me out of this cave?" Elizabeth said between clenched teeth.

"Just answer the question and you can go anywhere you want," Bruce responded in a low voice.

"Do you *want* to die out here? For once we're going to use some common sense," Elizabeth said angrily.

"I see you've dubbed yourself Queen of Common Sense," Bruce sneered.

"Don't start on her, she's right," Todd snapped, suddenly appearing behind Bruce in the cave entrance.

"Oh, look, the Thought Police have arrived," Bruce said sarcastically.

Elizabeth closed her eyes. She counted to ten, wishing all of this would disappear. When she opened her eyes again, she saw Todd and Bruce staring at each other. The muscles in Todd's neck were as taut as ropes.

"Bruce, please," Elizabeth whispered. "We've got to stick together." Something in his cold blue eyes softened. For an instant she saw a flicker of fear and vulnerability in his face.

"You can't win this round, Patman," Todd added. Elizabeth winced. She wished Todd had resisted the temptation to throw a final insult.

"We'll see who wins," Bruce said in a low voice.

He backed off and made room for Elizabeth to pass. As she stepped outside into the rapidly warming air, she looked back over her shoulder at Todd and Bruce. Todd had turned his back to Bruce and begun walking out of the cave. With a shiver Elizabeth saw Bruce's eyes narrow into a hard look as he followed Todd.

She unzipped the side pocket of her pack and took out her compass and map. The driving thunderstorm of the night before was history. The worst of the journey to the Oasis had to be behind them now.

"According to my calculations, we head down the trail and due north," Elizabeth announced. She

32

folded up the map and wrote the compass numbers in a small logbook. "Let's go."

"That's music to my ears," Jessica said, slathering sunscreen on her sunburned arms. "I wish I had my headphones right now. Some good music would get me through this huge outdoor sauna faster." Jessica ignored her sister's indulgent look and snapped the top shut on her lotion. Then she began humming her favorite Jamie Peters song, swaying to an imaginary beat.

"What on earth are you doing, Jess?" Elizabeth asked, putting her compass back in its black leather case.

"While you're busy being a Girl Scout, what's wrong with my drumming up some fun for myself?" Everyone was getting so serious and boring. And she had to agree with Elizabeth that the fighting between them really *was* getting kind of dangerous.

"Wakefield, they ought to put you in a special exhibit at the zoo," Bruce observed.

"Hey, don't knock it until you've tried it," Jessica said, still rocking her torso from side to side. Bruce shook his head and grinned wearily. "See, I even got you to crack a smile," she added. *I'm not going to let anything get to me for the last few hours of this awful trip,* she thought with a surge of positive energy.

"My ankle's better this morning, but not great. I'll be fine if someone can help me get to the trail," Heather said. Jessica glanced at Heather's slender leg and fantasized that it was crawling with red desert ants. Bruce was standing right next to Heather, but

33

he shrugged indifferently. Todd threw Bruce a sharp look of disapproval. "Heather, I'll help you out," Todd offered.

"Heather and I have got this down to a science," Ken said, clapping a bronzed hand on Todd's shoulder. Jessica felt the temperature rise in her face as she watched Ken offer his arm to Heather. Heather daintily clasped it, as if this were prom night, and tottered along, glued to Ken's arm. *How can they walk that slowly without falling asleep standing up?* Jessica stormed past them down the trail to catch up with Elizabeth, Todd, and Bruce.

"So how much do we have left of this fabulous adventure?" Jessica flippantly asked Elizabeth as she tied her cotton T-shirt into a knot above her midriff.

"I measured the map pretty carefully," Elizabeth said. "And I'd guess twenty-five miles—about two full days of walking."

"Two days?" Todd said, his jaw dropping.

"That's ridiculous. Let me see that," Bruce said, grabbing the map from Elizabeth. Jessica leaned over his shoulder and intently studied the route.

"Twenty-five miles," Jessica confirmed, raking a hand through her hair.

"Then let's really move it," Todd said.

"Hey, can't you guys go any faster?" Bruce called back to Ken and Heather with exasperation. "She's really slowing us down," Bruce added irritably, looking at Jessica. It comforted her somewhat that she wasn't the only one who was fed up with Heather.

"No can do," Ken called. "Heather's my official

trip buddy. I'm not going to push her faster than she can go. And I have to keep an eye on her."

"There's nothing more dangerous than loyalty," Bruce snorted, throwing his hands in the air.

Jessica rolled her eyes. *The magnificent buddy system strikes again.* Kay Jansen had paired the group into buddies back at SVSS, assigning Ken to buddy with Heather. Elizabeth had been paired with Bruce, and Jessica got stuck with Todd. Everyone but Ken had completely forgotten about the buddy system, but he certainly seemed to enjoy reviving it for the purpose of being Princess Mallone's knight in shining armor.

Jessica trudged sullenly up the dry trail. If they hiked at a normal speed, it would take them two whole days to reach Desert Oasis. But with Heather's snaillike pace, it could take them twice that long. Jessica felt a jolt of reality in the pit of her stomach.

"We can't hang around for three or four more days in the desert, you guys," she said, stopping short on the trail. "We don't have enough food."

Bruce, Todd, and Elizabeth stopped walking and looked at each other. Then all three of them looked back at Ken and Heather lagging behind on the trail.

"Jessica's right," Elizabeth sighed.

"Of course I'm right," Jessica snapped. "You should have listened to me and hiked out last night, instead of wasting valuable time." Jessica's resolve to stay in a good mood all day was rapidly disintegrating.

"There's nothing we can do about it except to keep going," Elizabeth said evenly. Jessica exhaled impatiently.

35

"It's only eight A.M. and warm already," Todd said, shielding his eyes and gazing out onto the distant horizon. "We need to keep hiking, before it gets too hot."

"I've had it with this moonscape," Jessica mumbled. "As soon as we get home, I intend to lounge around the pool for a week straight, drinking iced coffee."

"Speaking of iced coffee, how much water do we have?" Elizabeth asked, examining her bottle.

"About half a bottle," Todd said, holding up his canteen.

"Same here," Bruce answered.

"I'm almost down to the bottom of mine," Jessica said, unconcerned. Why should she be worried? Didn't it rain buckets the night before? They'd be running into pools of fresh rainwater as soon as they got to the bottom of the trail.

"But you had more than half a bottle yesterday morning," Elizabeth said in alarm.

"Why are you having such a cow?" Jessica retorted. Elizabeth always got herself worked up over the most unnecessary things. "Did you notice it rained enough last night to flood the Mississippi? I'll fill up my water bottle in the mountain runoff, no problem."

"Jess, have you *seen* any mountain runoff so far?" Elizabeth asked.

"No, but I will when we hike down lower," Jessica said with a shrug.

"Don't you remember what they said in basic survival training? Sudden desert rainstorms dry up right away, they don't leave nice pools of water," Elizabeth explained in a tone of resignation.

Jessica stared at her water bottle. *Terrific. I'll die of thirst before I starve to death.*

"Fine, so I made a mistake, it's been known to happen once or twice," Jessica said. "But this is an even better reason to pick up the pace on this hike. We're moving at a rate of an inch an hour. It will be March of the year 2000 before we get back to the Oasis."

"Heather *is* slowing us down," Todd conceded.

Bingo. Todd's really a genius when he has to be, Jessica thought disgustedly. She casually shook her water bottle before securing it to the belt of her backpack. The hot, white sun was rising higher in the sky. But she felt a chill of fear rush through her limbs.

"We're in agreement that Heather's seriously holding us up," Jessica said, trying to keep her voice calm. "So what are we going to do?"

"We're stopping by the big sage bushes up ahead for a conference," Elizabeth called back to Ken.

Ken nodded. He took Heather's elbow and helped her climb up the short incline to the spot shaded by the sage cluster. Jessica watched Heather flop onto the scratchy ground and fluff out her hair, lifting her face to the sun. Did she think they were settling in for an afternoon at Club Med? *Maybe a large hawk'll come along and carry Heather off, solving all our problems at once,* she thought.

Bruce, Ken, and Todd pushed aside rocks and

small cacti and found places to sit down.

"OK, we need to make a decision," Elizabeth said. "I understand that Heather's having a lot of trouble walking. But we've got to speed up and get to the Oasis by tomorrow night at the latest, or we'll be facing real jeopardy. Anybody have a suggestion?"

"We could take turns carrying her piggyback," Ken offered.

"And what would you do with your backpack and both of your sleeping bags—hold them in your teeth?" Bruce asked.

"We could distribute our stuff, which isn't that much, in everyone else's packs. And then I'd carry her," Ken said. Carry the Queen of Sheba across the entire desert? *Quel romantique.* Jessica had never heard of anything so ludicrous in her entire life.

"You can't carry her for twenty-five miles," Jessica pointed out, trying to sound as diplomatic and helpful as she could. "So why don't you and Todd and Bruce trade off carrying her?"

"No way, José," Bruce said blandly, lying down with his arms crossed over his eyes.

"She probably only weighs about a hundred twenty pounds," Todd said.

"I do not weigh anything *close* to a hundred twenty pounds," Heather objected sharply.

"OK, a hundred pounds, a thousand pardons. It's still impossible. Our packs alone feel like they're filled with bowling balls, and they only actually weigh about twenty-five pounds," Bruce said in a wooden voice.

"We're going around in circles," Jessica said wearily. "Whatever we're going to do, let's just do it."

"Well, there's only one solution, as I see it," Elizabeth said finally. "We'll have to leave Heather in a sheltered place and send help on Saturday."

"Great idea," Jessica said brightly. *Finally, we're going to dump Heather!* "Well, then let's go," Jessica said, ignoring Heather's stare. She jumped up energetically and brushed herself off.

"Hold it, we can't leave Heather alone out here," Todd pointed out. "One of the guys should stay here with her until a rescue squad can be sent."

"I don't mind staying, but I really wouldn't feel safe alone out here," Heather agreed.

"I know," Elizabeth said thoughtfully, raising an eyebrow. "Jessica, instead of complaining for the next two days, why don't *you* stay behind with Heather?"

Jessica stopped short. She pondered the options: Would she rather walk twenty-five miles in the blistering sun, or sit in the shade with her most hated rival? It was a tough call. But not that tough. She'd rather do *anything* besides spend one unnecessary minute with Heather.

"Forget it," Jessica said with finality. "I'm going with you."

"Since Ken is Heather's buddy, he should stay with her," Todd said. Heather grinned at Ken, who gave her a light pat on the shoulder. Jessica froze. That stupid buddy system! Jessica could tell exactly what was going on in Heather's slimy little mind.

"On second thought, I'm pretty burned out. And I

39

don't have much water. Maybe I better stay with Heather, after all," Jessica said breezily.

"Fine," Elizabeth said, raising an eyebrow again at Jessica. "The rest of us should push off, then."

"Wait, we can't leave two girls alone here," Todd protested. "What if there really are three felons roaming around out here?"

"He's got a good point," Ken agreed. "Jessica, go on ahead. I'll stay here." Jessica watched him brush strands of blond hair away from his forehead. It seemed like years since she'd kissed him. Something hard closed around her heart. *I'll bet you're dying to get rid of the rest of us and be alone with her. Well, forget it.*

"What makes you think you'd act more sensibly in some dire situation than I would?" Jessica argued.

"I didn't say that, Jessica," Ken said, his blue eyes blazing. "I just—"

"Whatever happens, Jess can handle it," Elizabeth interrupted. "I have faith in her." Jessica gave Elizabeth a sideways look.

"Jessica's tough as shoe leather," Bruce said.

"Shut up, Bruce," Jessica responded good-naturedly.

"Yeah, I guess you're right," Ken said. He gazed softly at Jessica.

Jessica gave Ken a quick, taut smile. Then she quickly unzipped the side pocket of her pack and got out her tube of sunscreen.

"Hey, Liz, you're looking a little sunburned. Need some of this?" Jessica said loudly as she walked over to Elizabeth.

"What an unexpected act of kindness from my irritable sister." Elizabeth accepted the tube and rubbed the lotion onto her neck and shoulders.

"Thanks for helping me out," Jessica whispered. "Sometimes your annoying logic actually saves the day."

"Don't mention it. Believe it or not, I meant every word," Elizabeth whispered back. She handed the tube of lotion to her sister, then bent over to hoist her pack over her shoulders.

Jessica watched a group of wrens fly across the azure-blue sky—the color of Ken's eyes. She glanced over at Ken and felt a pang. She longed to run her fingers along the strong lines of his jaw.

She began to walk back toward him. If they could talk, just hold each other again, then everything would be all right. But suddenly Ken got up and sat down again not more than an inch away from Heather. He began speaking in low tones to her, intently making sure she was clear on emergency procedures. Heather dumbly batted her eyelashes as Ken talked. Jessica felt jealousy grasping at her heart again. *Can I ever forgive Ken for betraying me?* she wondered.

"We'll send a rescue team out the second we get to the Oasis," Elizabeth said, buckling the strap of her backpack tight around her hips. The rest of the gang was already loaded up and ready to head down the trail.

"You two be sure you get some sleep tonight. Don't party too late," Bruce advised.

"Hey, how do you know a tall, dark stranger won't

41

appear and sweep me off into the night?" Jessica said, catching Ken's glance out of the corner of her eye.

"That's exactly what we're afraid of," Todd said with a concerned look on his face.

"Not to worry," Jessica answered with a wave of her hand. "I'm sure this will be a very uneventful evening."

Elizabeth hoped Jessica was right. She stared off at the mountain peaks in the distance, beyond the miles of flat, salt-encrusted ground, and wondered if any unknown dangers lurked beyond her line of vision.

"Jess, why don't you hang on to the granola bar rations for you and Heather?" Elizabeth said, passing a package of peanut-butter bars to Jessica.

"Just what I've been craving! It's been so long since I've had a granola bar," Jessica said sarcastically, accepting the package and slipping it into her pack.

"And how about a little more water, just in case?" Elizabeth added, pouring a quarter of her bottle into Jessica's. "It's not much, but you can drink small mouthfuls at a time. It's enough to keep you alive."

"Thanks, Liz. I can't think of anyone I'd rather share this horrendous, life-threatening experience with than you," Jessica said.

"You better be the keepers of the flare, too," Todd said, pulling the red tube from his pack and handing it to Jessica.

"That's the only one we have," Bruce pointed out.

"But Todd's right," Elizabeth concurred. "Jessica and Heather are the ones who need it. In an emergency we could run to them a lot faster than they could get to us."

"Don't use it unless you're in a really dangerous situation," Ken said. Heather nodded soberly. Elizabeth didn't even want to imagine how she'd feel if she actually saw the orange smoke rising into the sky.

"Did you think we'd set it off for kicks?" Jessica asked Ken testily. Elizabeth rolled her eyes. *Can't they carry out one simple procedure without getting on each other's nerves?* she thought.

"Jessica, this is serious, why can't—" Ken started.

"Cut!" Elizabeth yelled, drawing an imaginary line across her throat. "Save your arguments for when we get home. Right now, let's get going." Ken shifted uncomfortably, tucking his T-shirt into his shorts.

"I know you'll do great whatever happens," Ken said quietly to Jessica.

"Thanks," Jessica answered. Elizabeth noticed that Jessica didn't move to kiss Ken good-bye.

Elizabeth, Ken, Todd, and Bruce trudged down the craggy slope of the trail. Elizabeth looked up at a prairie falcon circling overhead and then back over her shoulder. *I hope we've done the right thing, leaving Jess out here alone.* If anything went wrong, Elizabeth knew Heather wouldn't be able to help—it would all be up to Jessica. Elizabeth felt a strange twinge in her stomach. *We've got to hurry to the Oasis and get them out of here fast.*

Chapter 4

Elizabeth, Bruce, Todd, and Ken continued forging across the scorching desert. Shimmering heat waves danced before them over the sand.

"These cactus spines keep stabbing my ankles," Bruce said, plucking tiny spikes off his socks.

"Me, too," Todd said, rubbing the calves of his legs. Elizabeth wished that the sharp teeth of the cacti was their worst problem. She looked up into the glare of the midday sky.

"I think I'm going to melt into lizard food," she said wearily. In the cooler hours of the morning their task seemed relatively simple: hike to the Oasis and send help back to Heather and Jessica. But as the sun beat down on her, Elizabeth was increasingly aware of her thirst and hunger. Just reaching the Oasis would be a miracle.

Todd pulled out an SVH baseball cap and placed the visor firmly over his brow. "Liz, you're going to pass out from the heat if you don't put something on your head," he said.

"I guess we don't need another disabled person on this trip," Elizabeth answered. She tied an Indian-print bandanna around her head to act as a sweat-band, and to keep her from getting baked.

"You've both definitely got the right idea," Ken agreed, reaching back to fish around in his own pack. He came up with a blue-and-white sailor's cap, which he pressed onto his sun-bleached blond hair.

"You look ready for the high seas," Todd observed.

"Aye, aye," Ken laughed. Elizabeth watched Ken as he put on his sunglasses. They accentuated his tanned good looks.

"Bruce, are you going for an Olympic record in heat endurance, or do you want a hat?" Todd said, offering Bruce a wide-brimmed canvas fishing cap. Bruce glanced disdainfully at the offering.

"Hats are for geeks, Wilkins. Or maybe you already knew that." Bruce tossed off.

"Is that right? Maybe we can discuss it at leisure when you're in the hospital, recovering from massive heat stroke," Todd said tightly.

"I don't think so," Bruce answered smoothly. "Unlike you wimps, I can handle the sun."

"You know, Patman, much to my astonishment, I was almost beginning to enjoy your company. But I could change my mind at any time," Todd said.

"Hey, is that some kind of threat?" Bruce asked with a sharp laugh. Elizabeth ignored them. She'd gotten used to the fact that this brittle bantering would go on until the whole horrible trip was over.

They hiked on for an hour in the rising heat.

"I could use a two-minute break," Bruce finally said. He stopped walking and leaned heavily against a large rock.

"You're not getting worn out from the heat, are you, Bruce?" Todd asked.

"I'd say two minutes of rest an hour hardly constitutes being worn out," Bruce answered. He stood up straight and placed his hands on his hips.

"Patman, you're so full of—"

"Maybe we all could use a break," Elizabeth observed, cutting Todd off.

"I could use another half a granola bar," Bruce said. He removed the cap from his water bottle and threw his head back to drink. He carelessly let water drip from the bottle down his neck. Elizabeth looked into his sunburned face and shook her head.

"We have another day and a half of walking and only one granola bar left for each of us—half for tonight and half for tomorrow," she reminded Bruce.

"Oh, right, I forgot the rules," Bruce said. He didn't even seem to have the energy for his usual level of sarcasm.

"Where's your stamina, Patman?" Todd asked, lowering his pack to the ground. "You've played plenty of tennis games under the glaring sun at country clubs."

Bruce capped his water and stared directly at Todd. Elizabeth felt her breath catch. "Todd, could you possibly be jealous because the Patman wealth and sophistication go back generations and your father's success is, well, *nouveau*?" Bruce asked slowly.

Elizabeth instinctively touched Todd's arm. She felt him flinch from Bruce's insult.

"My father is a very hardworking man," Todd said through clenched teeth. "And by the way, I'd say *your* generations of Tahitian vacations and four-story mansions are doing you about as much good out here as these stupid bags of gold."

Elizabeth couldn't ignore them any longer. Bruce and Todd were starting to break out the heavy artillery. They could declare war at any moment.

"Well, I'm feeling much better! Why don't we start up again?" Elizabeth asked cheerfully, dragging Todd away from Bruce and back toward the trail.

"Look, a desert tortoise," Ken said, pointing toward a patch of dried brush about twenty yards off the trail. Elizabeth watched the green shell lumbering along on squat legs. It was a relief to see some life in the desert, even if it was a reptile.

They crossed a dry riverbed and followed the trail as it curved around a bend of spectacular red rock, which provided much-needed shade. Elizabeth was so awed by the jagged beauty of the towering rock face that she almost forgot how sore her back and feet were. Even Bruce and Todd were walking quietly, keeping a safe distance from one another. She glanced at Todd, who looked as awestruck by the stark landscape as she. As long as they kept moving and didn't have to talk to each other, maybe Todd and Bruce wouldn't start fighting again.

"Uh-oh, do you see what's ahead?" Ken asked as the curve in the rock straightened out.

"It looks like a fork in the trail," Elizabeth said. "I don't remember seeing one on the map this morning. I hope we're on the right track."

The four of them stopped walking. If they took the left fork, they would remain on low ground all the way along the canyon floor. If they took the fork to the right, it would mean climbing high up to a hilly crest. Elizabeth squinted at the upper trail. They'd be able to walk only part of the way and would have to climb the rest up a sheer rock slope. They'd been taught basic climbing safety in the SVSS training seminar—and had also been explicitly cautioned about its dangers.

She knelt at the point where the trail split and laid the map out on the ground, pinning down the corners with rocks.

"There, I see the fork," Todd said. "It obviously doesn't matter which way we go, the trails converge down here." He pointed to a location on the map a few miles farther.

"So let's stay on the lower trail," Bruce said, scanning the upper trail on the map. "Unless you're in the mood for heroics."

"How do you know it doesn't matter? We can't tell from the map which choice is better," Elizabeth remarked, looking up at Todd.

"OK, I don't know. So let's take the trail that's obviously easier," Todd said.

"Todd, slow down. We really have to think about this," Elizabeth said.

"What's wrong with skipping all this rumination and taking the left fork?" Todd demanded impatiently.

Rumination? He made it sound as if Elizabeth were sitting in the air-conditioned safety of a library, poring over English poetry.

"I can tell you what's wrong with it—" Elizabeth began.

"Fine, I'm all ears," Todd said, cutting her off in a clipped tone. In the past Todd had always been willing to listen to Elizabeth's reasoning and trust her instincts. Why was he trying to pick a fight with her now?

"All right. That storm we had last night could have been a preview of the real thing," Elizabeth said. "And if the real thing comes and we're on low ground, we could be swept away in a flash flood."

"That storm looked pretty real to me," Todd said. He stood up, brushed the dust off his legs, and walked back toward his pack.

Elizabeth remained crouched over the map, aching from the sting of his rejection. But she had a gut feeling that she was right, and she wasn't going to give in.

If we all die in a flash flood, Elizabeth thought grimly as she folded the map, *it won't matter who was right.*

"You're crazy," Bruce told Elizabeth. "You'd have to be a mountain goat to climb that trail. Besides, going up will add a day to the trip. That'll mean another whole day without any food at all."

"But we'll get there *alive*," Elizabeth argued. "We can hunt for lizards and snakes. People have managed to survive in the wilderness before."

"And how do you plan to do that? Spear them with your pocketknife?" Bruce asked.

"Exactly," Elizabeth returned.

Todd hiked on, the sound of Elizabeth and Bruce snapping at each other grating on his nerves. Sticking his fingers in his ears, unfortunately, failed to block out the sound of their argument. Usually Elizabeth's voice was as soothing to him as cool water, but he was so irritated now that every word she said was like fingernails scraping across a blackboard.

"Bruce, you can eat *toads* for all I care. The point is that if we're in that canyon and get another fifteen minutes of driving rain, the entire subject of food will be *moot*," Elizabeth said. Todd cringed at the shrill edge in her voice.

"Elizabeth, I need to say something to you, and I don't want you to take it the wrong way," Todd said, pulling his fingers out of his ears and massaging his throbbing temples.

"What?" she asked.

"You know that I've always admired the sensible way you present your side of an argument. . . ." Todd began.

"Thanks, Todd," Elizabeth said with surprise. She smiled gently.

"But you've made your point. So right now I

wish you'd stuff a sock in it," Todd answered.

Elizabeth's mouth fell open in shock, and then her face crumpled.

"Liz, I just mean—"

"Forget it, I know what you mean," Elizabeth said quietly, wiping aside a tear. "Sometimes you're almost as bad as Bruce." She walked along silently.

"Clear skies as far as the eye can see, Wakefield," Bruce reported, pivoting around with his arms spread wide, to take in the panorama of scenery. "Proof that chances of showers anytime in the next week are less than zero percent."

"Bruce, you've reached new heights of egomania—astounding even for you. You can outguess the weather," Elizabeth said.

"Elizabeth, lighten up a little. I know why you're mad at me, but can't you even take a joke?" Todd said impatiently.

"Todd, does this look like a comedy club?" Elizabeth snapped.

"Do you think you could manage for one second to get that tone of superiority out of your voice?" Todd asked Elizabeth flatly. He threw off his pack and sat down. Todd looked up and saw that Elizabeth was standing over him with a stricken look on her beautiful face.

"I'm sorry, Todd," Elizabeth said, her voice quivering.

"OK," he answered softly. He looked up at her. Elizabeth's sensitive blue eyes were wide with fear.

Todd knew that Elizabeth really believed they

52

might get hit by a flash flood if they took the lower route. But he also thought she should get off her high horse. She was acting as if she'd spent the last twenty years trailblazing through Death Valley and was some kind of an expert.

Maybe the right thing for Todd to do was to show support for Elizabeth's concerns and follow the trail she wanted to take. But he had his own concerns, too. *And for once, I'm going to put those first,* he decided. As much of a jerk as Bruce was, Todd had to agree with his basic point. There wasn't a cloud to be seen anywhere. Just a flat blue sky.

"I say we take the lower fork," Todd said decisively, retying his bootlaces. Elizabeth was staring at him, and he knew that he'd hurt her again. But that couldn't be helped. "Liz, it looks like it's rained itself out. We have to get to the Oasis as soon as we can to send help back to Heather and Jessica."

"First time you've made sense on this entire trip, Wilkins," Bruce commented.

"And there's one other factor," Todd went on, ignoring Bruce. "We could exhaust ourselves taking the uphill route—and end up unidentified skeletons in the desert." The image of those six dusty skeletons in the cave, with their hollow, eyeless stares, rose eerily in his mind.

Todd glanced over at Ken, who hadn't contributed a single word to the entire debate. He was standing off by himself, apparently contemplating the scrubby sand between his boots. *Ken probably realizes that the only sane choice is to take the lower fork and doesn't see the point in arguing about it,* Todd thought.

"What do you think, Ken?" Todd asked in a businesslike tone.

"I have to go along with Elizabeth on this," Ken said quietly, sitting on a large rock and resting his elbows on his thighs.

"Here we go again," Bruce groaned.

"I want to hear Ken out," Elizabeth said, holding her palm up to silence Bruce. Todd looked out at the barren sand dunes, which were corrugated with wind ripples. *Whatever his reasons are, they better be good,* he thought.

"I saw a film once with a desert flash flood," Ken said, rubbing his thumb across the moss on the underside of a rock. "It's really stayed with me." Elizabeth sat down on the ground and drew her legs up to her chest, watching Ken. There was something about her rapt interest that annoyed Todd.

"What happened?" Elizabeth asked.

"What you'd expect," Ken said with a shrug. "Some people were hiking along, it started to rain, then *wham*—in a matter of minutes they were trapped."

"So your vote is to stick to the high ground," Todd said, trying to move things along.

"Sounds like it was an incredible movie. Sometimes powerful film images haunt me for weeks," Elizabeth said, locking her gaze on Ken.

"Oh, I know," Ken agreed. "Have you seen the one that's playing at the Sweet Valley Cinema right now?"

"Not yet," she said, shaking her head.

"You'd really like it," Ken said, not taking his eyes from Elizabeth's.

Todd watched Elizabeth push her fingers through her silky, uncombed hair. Ken and Elizabeth were chatting together in their own world as if Todd and Bruce didn't even exist. Of course, everyone always talked to Elizabeth about everything.

In fact, she always listened to everyone as if he or she were the most important person in the world. Todd loved the fact that Elizabeth had so many friends. So why did he feel his stomach twisting into angry knots as he watched her and Ken talking? *Ken is my best friend,* he reminded himself. *Why shouldn't she talk to him?*

But Todd knew that Elizabeth had dated Ken in secret while he'd been living for a few months in Vermont. After Todd had returned to Sweet Valley, Jessica had started going out with Ken, and Elizabeth had pulled a twin switch to be with him one last time. When Jessica had found out about that, she'd spilled the beans to Todd. Elizabeth and Todd had almost broken up for good.

But Elizabeth convinced me that the switch made her realize how much she really loved me, Todd remembered. They had been able to mend their relationship, and Todd had believed that the ordeal was behind them. Now, out here in the desert, with the sun beating down and Elizabeth paying so much attention to Ken, he wasn't sure what he believed anymore. He shook his head.

"Ken and I refuse to take the lower trail," Todd heard Elizabeth say.

"Well, guess what, you can count me out of the upper one," Bruce said, tossing a stone out over the sand.

"So should we stand here and argue about it until the next ice age?" Todd said, glowering.

"I say we split up. We can meet later—if our paths cross," Bruce said. He readjusted his pack and turned to leave.

"Suits me," Ken said, gazing down the lower trail and shivering, despite the scorching temperature.

"But it's miles until the trails come back together," Todd pointed out. "If we split, we'll have to camp separately tonight. And that might not be safe."

"And you have a better solution?" Bruce asked, staring at the sunlight reflecting off his open pocket-knife.

Todd gazed out at the gray and camel-colored mountains in the distance. "No," he murmured.

"Hey, Matthews," Bruce yelled to Ken and Elizabeth as they started up the right fork. "Don't do anything I wouldn't do."

Todd wheeled around to see Bruce winking as Ken and Elizabeth blushed furiously. Todd's stomach twisted. He glared up at Ken and Elizabeth. *Those two have awfully guilty looks on their faces,* he thought.

"Be careful, Todd," Elizabeth called down from the upper trail. "I'll see you soon, OK?"

Todd looked up into her open, smiling face. He

felt a rush of love and trust for Elizabeth. She would never do anything to hurt him again. *I've got to get a grip. What is this trip doing to me?*

"Move it, Wilkins! I'm waiting," Bruce called up from the lower trail. He was standing with his hands on his hips, his face set in a smirk.

For what seemed like the hundredth time in the last few days, Todd remembered the terrible brief time when Elizabeth and Bruce had been drawn together. Convinced that Mr. Patman and Mrs. Wakefield were having an affair, Bruce and Elizabeth had sought comfort in one another.

Unfortunately, giving each other comfort had included passionate kisses. Todd forced out of his mind the horrible memory of finding Bruce and Elizabeth wrapped in each other's arms in the Wakefield's kitchen. He shuddered—that had been one of the worst moments he'd ever had to live through.

As Todd walked slowly toward the desert trail, he felt something wild and emotional well up inside him. He wanted nothing more than to throttle Bruce within an inch of his life.

Chapter 5

Jessica unlaced her boots to massage her sore feet and glared at Heather, who was sitting on the other side of the campground. *This truly takes the cake! I can't believe I'm stuck in the middle of nowhere with the person I hate most in the world.* They hadn't spoken a word to each other in hours.

Heather broke the silence. "I feel like I've had a hair dryer blowing in my face all day," she said, puffing her cheeks out and exhaling in a deep sigh. "At least the sun is going down and it's getting a little cooler." She picked up Elizabeth's red plaid shirt from the ground and slipped her arms into it.

Jessica groaned to herself. She should have guessed it was too much to ask to be spared Heather's whining voice much longer. *So what are we going to do now, discuss the weather?* she wondered irritably.

Heather untied her own shoes and pulled a sock

off a manicured foot. Jessica stared with scorn at the custom-made cheerleading shoes that Heather had worn instead of regulation hiking boots. True, the heavy steel-tipped boots weren't exactly Jessica's idea of top fashion either—she couldn't wait to slip back into a pair of oiled Italian sandals. But at least she had brains in her head instead of cobwebs. Well, if she was reduced to talking to Heather for lack of any nearby intelligent life-forms, she might as well note Heather's idiocy and rub it in.

"So, Heather, have your *custom-made* cheerleading shoes helped you on this trip, like they did at Nationals? As I recall, you predicted they would," Jessica asked casually. Heather had been rubbing her blistered feet with a pained look on her face.

"I'd say they've brought me a little luck," Heather responded coolly. "I certainly slept safe and sound last night next to Todd . . . and Ken."

"Don't bother taking that as much of a victory," Jessica responded without missing a beat. She wasn't about to let Heather see how her comment had hit home. "He felt sorry for you."

It was bad enough that Jessica had been forced to cooperate with Heather in the statewide cheerleading competition, then, horribly, to put up with her for four days in the middle of a scorching desert. But now—now it was truly revolting that she actually was supposed to *protect* the girl. *I'd rather feed her to the lizards,* Jessica thought darkly.

That remark about Ken was an especially low blow. They'd obviously spent enough time in the desert for Heather to start fitting in: Heather seemed more like a scorpion every time Jessica looked at her.

Jessica's thoughts turned to Ken. She recalled their first kiss, standing in the ocean surf on a dark night, his arms encircling her. He'd often told her how she kept him preoccupied with thoughts of her day and night. But since this trip she doubted he'd given her a single thought for hours!

Heather unzipped a pocket of her jacket and took out a nail file. In the middle of Death Valley, she began filing her nails. Jessica stared at her in disbelief.

"Would you get real?" Jessica snorted. "What do you think—we're going to head down to the Beach Disco for some action later?" *I can't wait to get back and tell this one to Lila,* Jessica thought incredulously.

With a defiant toss of her head Heather stood up, then let out a shriek of pain and sat back down heavily. Jessica rolled her eyes. This tortured-ankle crisis was starting to get old.

"Don't fall! Might break a nail!" Jessica gasped with mock concern.

"Can't you see I'm in pain?" Heather said with a sob.

Jessica sighed. "Listen, why don't you help me start a campfire?" she asked. "It'll take your mind off your stupid foot."

"Obviously, I can't kneel down to do that without going into spasms of agony," Heather said sharply.

Jessica eyed Madame Prima Donna gripping her

useless ankle. "You know, Heather, if I were you, I might consider checking my snotty attitude at the door for one night of my life. You might even show a little gratitude," Jessica suggested calmly.

"Thank *you* for the fire you'd better make, because I can't do it," Heather said shrilly.

Jessica stared at the girl. Her yellow hair was sticking out like broom straws, her eyeliner was smudged all over her face, and she had bags under her eyes. She looked pathetic.

"Heather, I've got some interesting news for you," Jessica began. She knelt down next to Heather so they were face-to-face. "Your cashmere sweaters are currently dissolving in a canyon in Death Valley. You're lucky my sister is a sap and gave you a shirt so you wouldn't freeze—it's more than I would do. Our group has split up because you can't walk. Basically, I don't think you're in any position to make demands at all."

Heather's haughty little pout melted into a moody, distracted expression. She put her nail file away in her jacket pocket, rested her arms across her thighs, and leaned her chin on her fists.

Good, that shut her up. Jessica gathered sticks and brush, then confidently built a fire, eyeing Heather warily all the while. Jessica soon noticed her wiping a tear from her cheek.

As dusk fell and the temperature dropped, they huddled on top of flat rocks close to the fire. Jessica took out their dinner-ration granola bar, broke it in half, and handed Heather her piece.

"Oatmeal raisin, my favorite," Heather said, without a hint of sarcasm. "Thanks."

"Don't mention it. Specialty of the house," Jessica responded flatly. They ate in silence.

After dinner Jessica retrieved her brush from her backpack and began to brush her hair.

"Jessica?" Heather ventured quietly.

"Yes?" Jessica said impatiently, putting the brush away.

"Can I borrow your hairbrush?" Heather asked. "Just for a second?"

Jessica scowled at her. "How can I be sure you won't infest it with diseases?" she asked.

"I've felt so gross since I lost my shampoo and makeup. I'd feel a little better if I could brush my hair. You'd hate it if *your* hair was a total mess. Please, Jessica?"

"Oh, all right. It's annoying to watch someone beg—even you," Jessica conceded. She handed over her hairbrush, which Heather eagerly grabbed and began raking through her snarled mane.

"I'm so mad I lost my pack," Heather complained when she handed back the brush. She stared morosely into the fire. "I brought a good romance novel along. Now I don't have anything to do."

"I'm actually bored enough to write in my diary," Jessica said. She stirred the fire with a stick and threw on more sagebrush. The flames shot into the air and cast wavering light onto the campsite. Jessica reached into her pack and got out her diary and a ballpoint pen. She leaned back against a rock and opened the book. A few minutes passed in silence.

"Jessica?" Heather said.

"What do you want to borrow now, Mallone?" Jessica asked irritably, without looking up.

"Could you spare one page from your journal?" Heather asked in a small voice. Jessica glared at her. "Just one?" Heather asked. She gazed at Jessica with large eyes. She looked small, grungy, and lost.

"Sure." Jessica shrugged. She tore two sheets of paper out of her book and handed them to Heather, along with a felt-tip pen. Then she settled back to her own writing.

Jessica's Journal Entry
Friday Night

I can't think of anything worse than spending a Friday night alone with Heather. I should be out wearing a fabulous new black miniskirt with a silk purple top, and dancing with Ken. I'm so bored right now I could scream. Maybe some totally gorgeous guy will accidentally parachute into the campsite. At least I don't have to put up with Heather making a fool out of herself flirting with Ken anymore.

I wish Ken were here. I can see his favorite constellation, but I can't remember the name of it. If he were here, he'd remind me. Then he'd kiss me, a long, soft kiss. I'd give anything to know what he's thinking right now.

Jessica closed her book and capped her pen. She hugged her knees to her chest and gazed up at the stars. Then she closed her eyes and imagined Ken's face drawing closer to hers, bending toward her lips.

Heather's Journal Entry
Friday Night

I would give anything on earth to be soaking in an almond-oil bubble bath right now, or to have my portable TV back, or my sweaters— they cost a fortune. Well, I can easily replace the TV and the sweaters—it's only money. The one thing I'll never manage is to make Ken Matthews fall in love with me. He loves Jessica.

I can see why, though I'd die before I'd ever say it out loud or let anyone read this. She's prettier than I am. And I might be a better cheerleader, but she's got a lot of other things going for her that I'll never have. It almost makes me nauseated to think about it, but maybe someday Jessica and I will be reduced to becoming friends.

I feel really bad that I've slowed everyone down. I was so dumb to wear these shoes into the desert. I'm so scared about those convicts. No one believes me, but I saw those men out there. And mostly I'm afraid of starving to death and never getting home. I wish I could talk to my mother right now. She must be worried sick.

Heather put down the pen and read the pages she'd written. She folded them up and put them in her jacket pocket. A moment later she took them out again, scrunched them into a ball, and threw them into the flames. Staring pensively into the fire, she watched the pages burn to ash.

"What was that?" Heather suddenly said with alarm.

"What was what?" Jessica said blankly, looking into the fire. "I didn't hear anything."

"I swear I heard something in the brush out there," Heather said.

"Probably a fox or a badger," Jessica guessed.

"No, it sounded like footsteps. Like someone might be out there," Heather said, the pitch of her voice rising. "Would you please go check?"

The request was surprisingly polite. Maybe Jessica had made her point with Heather. Maybe Heather had finally learned not to cross her anymore. Jessica figured she might as well get up to check on the noise.

A few minutes later she came trudging back to the site. She hadn't seen or heard anything, not even a rabbit. Heather needed to get her hearing checked—and her head examined.

"Heather," Jessica called impatiently as she walked back. "I didn't see any—" Jessica froze when she reached the edge of the campsite. Heather was quickly tearing the wrapper off a bar of chocolate.

"You little snake!" Jessica shouted. "You didn't hear anything. You've been hoarding food and had to get me out of sight for a few minutes! You are such a lowlife, Mallone." She shook her head in disgust. "Not much for team spirit when it really counts, are you? If I told anyone on the cheerleading squad about this, your name would be mud in a matter of minutes!"

Heather froze still clenching the candy bar. "I just found it this second. I was going to share it with you," she said defensively.

"Right. And Jamie Peters called and begged me to sing on his next CD," Jessica scathingly replied.

"All right. I found it this morning and was saving it, I admit that," Heather confessed in a quiet voice. "But I did hear something. There's someone out there." Heather was a pretty good actress—Jessica had seen more than enough evidence of that. But there was an urgency in her voice now that sounded real.

"OK, so big deal, what if Godzilla himself is out there waiting to stomp us into pancake mix?" Jessica asked, her hands on her hips. "Do you want me to tell the squad what a chiseler you are in a life-and-death situation?"

Heather's face darkened. She broke her candy bar in half and handed a piece to Jessica.

They sat for a while, munching in silence. The extra rations, meager as they were, had softened Jessica's mood somewhat. She watched Heather staring into the fire.

"That half a candy bar really hit the spot," she said after a few moments.

"Yeah. Maybe one will suddenly materialize in *your* stuff tomorrow," Heather responded, her gaze fixed on the flames.

"Oh, I doubt that, but we can always hope," Jessica said thoughtfully. "Stranger things have happened."

"I guess we should get into our sleeping bags," Heather said unenthusiastically.

"I'm too tired to sleep," Jessica said.

"Yeah, me, too," Heather concurred sleepily. "Besides, the fire's really nice."

Jessica was suddenly very weary. "All I want to do is sit by the fire and not think about anything," she said. But as she sat huddled with Heather before the dying embers, the thought that something—or someone—was in the nearby brush wouldn't leave her. Both she and Heather had been avoiding the unspoken, unspeakable question on both their minds.

"What if there *are* escaped convicts prowling around out here?" Heather finally said. The question hung in the air.

For the first time since Heather had started whining about the escaped convicts, Jessica didn't brush aside her remark.

"Let's get into our bags and not think about it anymore tonight."

Jessica peeled off her sweatshirts and jacket and crawled into her sleeping bag. Heather got into hers and was snoring in seconds—but Jessica stared up at the night sky. *What if there really are three desperate criminals lurking out there in the darkness?* she wondered as she finally drifted off to sleep.

Jessica woke in the dark to a crunching sound on the gravel beside the campfire. With blurry vision she gazed at the last smoldering sparks in the fire and remembered where she was. Heather was still snoring. It was amazing how unglamorous Heather could be sometimes. Then Jessica heard it again: Something was walking in the brush and sand by the campsite. Her body went rigid. As she lay there trying to summon the courage to sit up and see what it was, she heard the distinct sound of someone unzipping a backpack.

The moon broke through the clouds, casting yellow light onto the campsite. Jessica's heart stopped. Three tall figures were hovering over the dying campfire. Two of them were standing, and one was rummaging through her backpack! *It's the escaped convicts!* she thought, horrified. *They're looking for the gold.*

Jessica shuddered. The men had probably stolen her gold nuggets in the first place! Would the convicts shoot her when they realized she didn't have any more?

Jessica wished she'd never even heard of gold. She'd give anything right now to be at home, trying to ignore her mother nagging her to wake up for school, rather than here, trying to will away dangerous convicts pawing through her belongings.

Jessica's blood pounded wildly in her ears. What

would the criminals do if they knew she was awake, watching them? If she moved one inch, her life could be over in an instant. *Go away,* she willed silently, *please just go away.* She nearly stopped breathing in an attempt to be completely still. *Please don't kill us.*

Just then Heather stirred.

"What time is it?" she asked sleepily. Jessica's stomach clenched at the sound of Heather's voice. She glanced at the men, who were too busy digging in her pack to have noticed Heather. *When you see them, pretend to be asleep and we'll be OK,* Jessica silently pleaded to Heather.

Finally, after what seemed like a lifetime to Jessica, Heather caught sight of the convicts. Instantly her eyes went wide and her mouth flew open in a scream loud enough to wake the skeletons they had left back at the cave. Jessica squeezed her eyes shut. Her heart was pounding. What would happen to them now?

"You're gonna wish you hadn't done that, little lady," a deep, menacing voice said in the dark.

Chapter 6

"Peaceful, isn't it?" Ken asked Elizabeth, his voice sounding strangely tender.

"It really is," Elizabeth agreed. She shifted uncomfortably on the rock she was sitting on. They were both quiet for a moment, looking out onto Death Valley from the high mesa.

"That trail was really steep," Ken added self-conciously.

"I know, I'm completely exhausted," Elizabeth said. Again, silence filled the air between them.

Elizabeth and Ken had finished setting up camp at dusk. Now they sat quietly, watching the sun set in a fiery red ball, orange and purple streaking across the sky. If only they could relax and enjoy what promised to be a spectacular sunset, Elizabeth thought. She and Ken had long since resolved any romantic tensions between them—at least that's what she had believed before they'd spent a night alone together in the middle of the desert!

"We need a campfire," Elizabeth announced a little too loudly.

"I'll give you a hand," Ken quickly offered. He jumped up and gathered scrub brush to set up the fire.

Elizabeth dived into her pack and pulled out a box of matches. She was grateful they both had something to do, sparing them the necessity of talking to each other.

Elizabeth was convinced that this rekindling of old feelings was her problem alone. Ken had obviously gotten over her completely. The incredibly special communication they'd once shared had changed into something less intimate now, though no less important. They were good friends. Elizabeth could feel Ken's gaze on her, but she concentrated on lighting the fire.

"It's going to take a minute for this fire to really get going," she said, blowing on the tiny flames. She still couldn't believe the extreme weather of the desert. The sun had barely set, and she was already turning into an ice cube. *I could use a sweatshirt right about now,* she thought.

Ken suddenly leaned over to Elizabeth's open pack and pulled out the sweatshirt that was sitting on top. As he handed it over to her, their fingers touched lightly for an instant. Elizabeth felt an unexpected current of electricity run straight up her arm.

"Thanks—you read my mind," she said. She laughed nervously, grateful that the darkness hid the rising color in her cheeks.

"I had a feeling you needed something warm to put on," Ken mumbled with a shrug.

Elizabeth shook out the sweatshirt. Then she noticed the logo and special colors. It was the Sweet Valley High sweatshirt Ken had given her at the start of the football season. That was when they'd first secretly fallen in love. Had he noticed when he handed it to her?

"Hey! Look at that!" Ken suddenly said, jumping to his feet.

"Where? What?" Elizabeth asked. She stood up frantically and looked out at the layers of orange, purple, and brown mountains now blending into one dark color as night fell.

"Look, another one, do you see that?" Ken said urgently, pulling Elizabeth around in front of him. He pointed to the sky and held her by one shoulder to steady her gaze.

"A shooting star," Elizabeth said with awe. She was acutely aware of Ken's hand on her shoulder as she watched the meteor rocketing across the clear sky.

"Shooting stars are really common in the desert," Ken explained excitedly.

"Maybe they happen as often back in Sweet Valley, but we don't bother to notice them," Elizabeth suggested. Her self-consciousness faded at Ken's warm hand resting on the base of her neck—it suddenly seemed like the most natural thing in the world. Elizabeth watched each sparkling diamond come out and wink at her in the cobalt-blue sky now

73

rapidly turned to velvet-black. Her deep fatigue seemed to melt away.

"Do you know what that range of mountains in the distance is called?" Ken asked.

"No, do you?" Elizabeth asked, surprised.

"Yeah. Funeral Mountains," Ken said.

"How eerie," Elizabeth said.

"I know what you mean," Ken answered. Elizabeth eased back against him, as he placed his hand on her arm. Even in the chill air she felt warmed by their innocent, platonic friendship. *And I'll keep telling myself that, over and over,* she vowed silently.

"Um . . . Jessica mentioned that you had a special interest in astronomy," Elizabeth stammered.

"Yeah, I love looking at the stars. I've studied all about them and read a lot of books," Ken said, bubbling with interest in the subject. "I can't believe how bright the Big Dipper is. And see that huge arc? That's Orion's belt." His hand slipped gently from her shoulder as he became absorbed in telling her what he knew about the night sky.

As Ken launched into an animated recitation about the constellations in the northern hemisphere, Elizabeth's memory wandered to the weekend afternoons they had spent together walking on the beach, talking for hours. Ken was still such a surprise to her. Astronomy! She'd thought she already knew all the corners of his mind, but here was a new one.

Elizabeth closed her eyes. She felt so much hope for their survival as she stood there on the mesa with

74

Ken. In spite of herself, she imagined Ken's arms around her, all the fears and tensions of the last few days dissolving, leaving her at peace.

Elizabeth shook herself from her reverie. Although it was nice that Ken was treating her so sweetly, she knew he was completely over what had happened between them in the past. But the warmth of his body against hers was hypnotizing. Elizabeth had to ease away from him before she ended up doing something embarrassing.

"Ken, I know I'm going to be hooked on stars for the rest of the trip and beyond," Elizabeth said softly. "But right now I need to sit by the campfire. I'm freezing."

"Good idea. I'm sorry—once I get started about stars, I forget about everything else. I should have realized you might be cold," Ken added considerately.

"No need to apologize," Elizabeth laughed. "It was fascinating. I just need to . . . uh . . . sit down, that's all." She eased herself onto a rock by the fire. Ken sat down facing her, about six feet away. Watching his face through the flames, Elizabeth wished she could understand the heat radiating from her heart, and the shiver running through the rest of her body.

"Why do you look so concerned back there?" Bruce called cheerfully over his shoulder to Todd as they walked into a campsite at sunset. "I bet you're thinking about Elizabeth. Don't worry. Ken's probably taking good care of her." He winked slyly at Todd, who felt ready to break Bruce's face in half.

"You're boring me, Patman," Todd said, setting his pack on the ground.

"Face it, Todd. Ken's a football star. He's also a pretty decent-looking guy, and he's into *sensitive* things like poetry. Girls like Elizabeth eat that stuff up. After what's probably going on between them tonight, I'd say you should forget her and start playing the field again," Bruce advised.

"You know, Bruce, maybe you should skip going into the family business and become a gallows hangman. For some reason, I think you'd really enjoy it," Todd said, trying to sound nonchalant. But deep inside, every comment Bruce uttered about Ken and Elizabeth made him all the more miserable.

"You're not trying to change the subject, are you?" Bruce said with mock amazement. "I'd think this one would be of particular interest to you. As I recall, Ken and Elizabeth looked *awfully* friendly during those long months you were in Vermont."

"That's over," Todd said with a shrug, despite his growing worry.

"Is that right? Well, *you* know that both the Wakefield girls are unreliable flirts," Bruce said confidentially.

"Oh? And how did you develop such an expert ability to judge?" Todd asked, matching Bruce's obnoxious banter blow for blow. He watched the sun set in orange and purple streaks. Maybe Bruce would get bored and go find some small, helpless desert creature to torture.

"Well, I have, in fact, kissed both girls myself," Bruce replied. "And between you and me, Todd, neither one is really that hot."

Todd was ready to blow a fuse. He furiously grabbed a handful of brush, gathered it into a pile, and lit a blazing campfire. He looked up the granite rock face towering above the campsite, and caught his breath. The canyon he and Bruce had hiked through must have been carved by treacherous, churning water.

Elizabeth had been so insistent about the risks involved in taking this lower trail. What if she turned out to be right? *I wish there would be a flash flood,* Todd found himself fantasizing. *I'd see it coming, but Bruce would be swept away, screaming.* It was a horrible thought, and Todd quickly banished it from his mind. *I have to get a grip! Everything Bruce is saying about Elizabeth is absolutely untrue.*

Ken sat opposite Elizabeth, watching her carefully tend the campfire. *I wonder if she ever thinks about the short time we were together. She probably doesn't even remember anymore,* he mused. He must have bored her to tears blathering on about astronomy. Elizabeth was no doubt completely over her old feelings for him.

He loved Jessica now. She had more spirit, energy, and fire than any person he'd ever met.

Ken had given Jessica a lot of tender, brotherly advice when she'd been going through her terrible times with Jeremy Randall. But now he recalled the first night he'd thought of Jessica as someone he could love—the night he'd kissed her, after the football game against Big Mesa, at a victory party on the beach.

All during that pivotal game he'd caught glimpses of Jessica leading cheers. Everyone in the crowded stadium had been carried away by her enthusiasm. They'd jumped to their feet to scream the cheers she'd led. They'd applauded her expert flips and jumps.

Just before Ken had thrown the final pass of the game, he'd glanced over at the cheering squad to see Jessica leap into a perfect split in the air as the crowd roared. With a surprising surge of energy, Ken had thrown the pass with all his might. They'd won the game.

Ken warmed his hands by the fire as it crackled quietly. His blood froze at the thought of anything happening to Jessica out in the desert tonight. But then he pictured her defiant face, her blazing blue eyes. She could take care of both herself and Heather. Jessica had a tendency to be self-centered— but in a tight spot she could be counted on to come through.

Elizabeth, on the other hand, never thought twice about helping people out. She was one of the most naturally generous people Ken knew. He looked over at her in the moonlight.

She had finished building up the fire, and Ken watched her take out her journal and start to write. Was she writing about him? He remembered how sweet Elizabeth's kisses were, how her face lit up when he'd surprise her with a single red rose, or a small book of poems. Their brief relationship had been a magic time. His gaze rested on her lips as she pressed the top of her pen to them in thought.

Ken decided he might as well take out his journal, too. He opened the book to a blank page and uncapped a pen. He gazed at the fire and then back at Elizabeth, who was too busy writing to notice him.

Ken's Journal Entry
Friday Night.

I keep thinking about the long walks I used to take with Elizabeth. The cool ocean breeze always tousled her silky hair as we talked. We parked in the evenings at Miller's Point, overlooking the twinkling city lights of Sweet Valley. When I kissed her, she let her head fall gently back against the headrest. Her warm body melted trustingly into my arms.

Ken stopped abruptly and crossed out what he had written. The intimacy he had once shared with Elizabeth Wakefield was over. So why was he unable to stop himself from reliving the memories?

"Just shut up about Elizabeth and Ken," Todd said. Bruce smiled ever so slightly, enraging Todd. But he didn't have the energy to fight back. He was exhausted from the day's hike.

The evening sky was turning from indigo-blue to black. Todd took a small sip from his water bottle, then held up the bottle to the firelight. It was only one-third filled with water. Hunger, thirst, and heat were slowly wearing down his confidence. He slumped on a rock by the fire and put his head in his hands. *Will I ever make it to the Oasis? Or will I die in Death Valley?*

"It's only getting to you because you know everything I'm saying is true." Bruce shrugged and threw more brush onto the fire. Todd felt the blood pound in his head.

"I said shut up," Todd responded weakly.

"Hey, toughen up, Wilkins. This survival trip was supposed to teach you some guts." Bruce shook his head with disdain. "You must feel like a failure."

Todd felt his chest constrict. Bruce's relentless badgering was eating him alive. He looked sharply into Bruce's narrowed eyes.

"Patman, the level of abuse you're dishing out is too much even for you," Todd finally said quietly. "I think you're losing your mind out here."

Bruce raised his eyebrows and curled his mouth into a horrible sneer. He started to speak, but then froze, staring at Todd's feet. A rattlesnake had slithered up next to the rock Todd was sitting on.

Todd saw it at the same time. "A rattlesnake," he whispered, his voice small with fear.

"Well, get out of the way, you idiot!" Bruce yelled. But Todd sat paralyzed.

Bruce quickly picked up a huge rock from the

ground and flung it at the rattlesnake. The snake sank back, stunned.

"Good move!" Todd yelled breathlessly, finally leaping up. "Let's toss him back into the brush before he snaps out of it." Todd moved his hand toward the snake's rattle, carefully avoiding the fanged head.

But before he could grab the snake by the tail, Bruce had picked up another rock and begun violently pounding its head. In minutes it was not only dead, but utterly pulverized.

Todd stared in horror at the grotesque pile of blood and snakeskin. He looked back up at Bruce, who had an expression of insane exhilaration on his face. Bruce was still holding the rock, which was covered with smashed snake guts. He smirked cruelly at Todd.

"Too bad you don't have what it takes to survive in the wilderness, Wilkins," Bruce said with cold eyes. "Leaves you at the mercy of anything."

Todd stared at the snake carcass and raked his hands through his hair. With exhaustion and defeat, Todd dragged out his sleeping bag and got into it without even bothering to take off his clothes. He lay miserably, staring at the cold stars, until he fell into an uneasy sleep.

Elizabeth glanced up at the yellow moon high over Death Valley. She adjusted the cotton shirt she'd placed over the hard boulder she was sitting on. Then she gazed back down at her journal.

Elizabeth's Journal Entry
Friday Evening

This seems like the first night in years that I haven't been worried about escaped convicts, or about how a bunch of skeletons died. I'm not even concerned about how we'll make it through the long, hot day tomorrow on half a granola bar each.

I feel so safe camping out on the mesa with Ken. Plus, it's great not to be arguing with anyone for a change! Todd was so critical when I misread the map and mistakenly miscalculated how close we were to that dangerous river. I'm glad I don't have to deal with his bad mood right now.

Ken, on the other hand, has been so patient through the whole ordeal of the trip. I have a terrible confession to make: Right now I want more than anything to go sit next to him. I want to touch his broad, handsome face and share a deep kiss. I can't believe I'm actually writing this!

As Elizabeth looked up from her journal, she was startled to find Ken's eyes on her. He was staring at her intensely, his face aglow from the campfire. She closed her book and put down her pen, returning his gaze steadily. *What am I doing?* she asked herself. *He's my sister's boyfriend.* But neither of them seemed to be able to break the spell.

"Elizabeth," Ken finally said, softly. In spite of herself, Elizabeth felt a thrill at the sound of her name.

"Yes?" she answered, holding her breath.

"Um . . . I discovered, believe it or not, that I actually have a deck of cards in my pack from the last time I went camping in the Sierras. Want to play gin rummy or something?"

"I'd love to," Elizabeth said with relief.

"Hey, pass the granola bar," Ken said, shuffling the deck.

"You bet," Elizabeth replied with a smile.

Elizabeth and Ken both got into their bags, facing each other. They propped Elizabeth's flashlight between them and organized their hands.

After an hour Elizabeth set her cards on the ground and rolled onto her back.

"I think I've had enough gin rummy and Go Fish to last me into the next century," Elizabeth said, stifling a yawn.

"I'm exhausted, too," Ken said. He gathered up the cards and put them back in their box.

"Good night," Elizabeth said quietly. She took off her sweatshirt and folded it into a pillow. Then she nestled down into her bag. She closed her eyes and took a deep, relaxed breath.

A moment later Elizabeth felt a long, soft kiss on her cheek. She heard Ken's voice whispering good night. Her stomach tightened. *Am I dreaming? Did he really kiss me?* Elizabeth considered sitting up, but instead she drifted off to sleep.

Chapter 7

"What are you talking about? That fork in the path obviously leads to high ground," Bruce said. He was following Todd up the salt-encrusted trail at the crack of dawn on Saturday morning.

Todd shot a glance at Bruce's haggard face, empathizing with his exhaustion. *But that doesn't change the fact that I can't stand him,* he reminded himself.

"Chill out, I'm following the map. It veers up for only a few hundred yards, then goes back down to the riverbed," Todd said, trying to control his rising anger. "Trust me."

Todd squinted up at the sun glaring over the barren canyon. He scanned the terrain on either side of the trail, in search of anything that might be edible. The only signs of vegetation were sharp cacti and a few tumbleweeds—nothing they could eat.

"Hey, move it, Todd. What's the matter, afraid of walking into another snake?" Bruce asked. "I bet a strong guy like *Ken* would have snapped that snake in two."

Todd felt his face grow hot. He glared at Bruce, thinking that his appearance would be vastly improved with a boa constrictor wrapped tightly around his neck.

"We need food and water, Patman," Todd said evenly, deciding not to let Bruce's insults get to him. "Look for a barrel cactus. The SVSS trainers said they contain water."

"What makes you think you can squeeze water out of a cactus, Wilkins?" Bruce said nastily. "You can barely read a map." Todd watched Bruce wipe dust from his face with the back of his hand. Despite Bruce's venom, Todd smiled to himself.

He knew exactly where they were and what the map said. Instead of veering back to the riverbed, their course would head directly for a rendezvous with Elizabeth and Ken. Although Todd would never allow Bruce to see the depth of his pain and confusion, he had become obsessed with the thought of Ken and Elizabeth together. Maybe there *was* nothing going on between them, and Bruce was just playing mind games. But Todd still had to see her. So what if it meant taking the higher trail for a few hours? If Todd kept Bruce distracted, he'd never notice the change of course.

"Bruce, you might not like the fact that we're stuck out here together, but your own negativity is going to drag you down," Todd said, taking a deep, slow breath. "So help me find a cactus, OK?"

"You know, maybe you're right," Bruce said, drawing out each syllable in a thoughtful tone. "As much as I think you're an utter wimp who couldn't navigate your way out of a paper bag—you're right. I really should think positively." Sarcasm dripped from his voice.

"Bruce, it's really amazing that someone as obnoxious as you has survived this long without someone knocking his teeth out," Todd said, sidestepping a rabbit hole.

"Try not to annoy me for a minute while I concentrate on finding water," Bruce said, placing the fingers of both hands on his forehead and squeezing his eyes shut. "I'm sensing water along a high trail."

"Good for you. Maybe you can read crystal balls for a living," Todd said, getting bored with Bruce's stupid antics.

"Aha! I see a vision of water," Bruce said, snapping his eyes open. "I see an oasis, a crystal-blue pool of water. I see two people slipping into the cool water."

"Cut it out, Bruce. This is hardly the time for jokes," Todd said, nervously retying his bootlace.

"It's Elizabeth and Ken," Bruce continued. "The water is tingling their hot skin. She has never looked more beautiful. I see him moving closer to her."

Todd fought every urge in his body to scream at Bruce to shut up. Despite the dry heat, his palms began to sweat. Against his will an image of Ken bringing his lips toward Elizabeth's swam before him.

No! Todd forced himself to shake off Bruce's spell. *What is he trying to do to me?*

"You have an active imagination, Patman," Todd said casually, determined to stop the core of his body from trembling. "How about imagining us our own oasis?"

As they turned a corner on the trail, Todd spied a barrel cactus. A surge of hope rose in him. "Get out your pocketknife and start chopping into the cactus with me," Todd called to Bruce.

"Do you really think we'll find water?" Bruce asked. Todd thought he detected the faintest glimmer of admiration in Bruce's curiosity. *This might turn the tables between us once and for all,* Todd thought.

He raised his knife above his head and hacked into the cactus. After several attempts it split wide-open. But Todd gasped as he saw only reedy, inedible pulp inside. Todd's heart pounded in his ears, drowning out Bruce's harsh laughter.

Suddenly all the jealousy and suspicion Todd had been trying to overcome rushed to the surface. He squeezed his eyes shut and imagined Elizabeth's beautiful face, her wise blue eyes. Whenever Elizabeth was sad or frustrated, she always wrote. Todd threw down his pack and knelt next to it in the dust. He opened the pack and pulled out his trip diary and a pen.

"What are you doing, Wilkins? Jotting down recipes for fresh cactus pulp?"

"No, taking notes for your funeral. I want it to be

a really special event," Todd shot back. He glared at Bruce and walked twenty yards off the trail. Todd sat down on a rock, opened his journal, and uncapped his pen.

Todd's Journal Entry
Saturday Morning

I don't know what's happening to me in this desert. I came out here to gain confidence, but instead my whole life is falling apart. I'm going crazy thinking about Liz camping alone with Ken last night. The thought of him kissing her is driving me insane. I'm totally ready to kill Patman. If he says one more word about Elizabeth, I'm going to wring his neck. I can't stand him.

My cactus idea was a bust and we're running out of water. I very possibly might die out here. All I know is that if this is the end, I have to see Elizabeth again before my life is over. No matter what else happens, I've got to tell her how much she means to me.

Elizabeth woke on Saturday morning and placed a hand over her eyes to block the already bright sun. Gently rolling to one side in her sleeping bag, she hit something soft and opened one eye to see what it was. She was snuggled against Ken! How did their sleeping bags get scrunched up so close together in the night?

89

Ken woke up and squinted at her, his lids still heavy with sleep. Then his eyes shot wide-open. For a charged split second they stared eye to eye.

"Um . . . did you sleep well?" Elizabeth asked, trying to free herself from the tangle of her bag.

"Great," Ken said quickly. He pulled his shirt on backward.

Elizabeth finally escaped from her bag and went to her pack, practically tripping over a jackrabbit that had hopped into their campsite. She ran a comb through her snarled blond hair.

All of Elizabeth's thoughts and feelings from the previous night came rushing back to her. She couldn't believe she almost took Ken in her arms! He must have sensed that she was about to, or he wouldn't have suggested out of the blue that they do something safe, like play cards. She snapped open the map.

"We've got about ten miles to go before we meet up with the others," Elizabeth said in a very businesslike tone.

"Elizabeth, can I tell you something?" Ken asked quietly.

"We may have some hard climbing ahead of us," Elizabeth went on, ignoring Ken. She was concentrating on the map with enough intensity to burn a hole through it.

"OK, but let's talk first," Ken said in the same gentle voice. Elizabeth's stomach did a double flip.

"If we keep a steady pace," Elizabeth continued, her words tumbling out, "we can reach the Oasis by late afternoon, and—"

"Elizabeth!" Ken said firmly, touching her forearm. "Slow down. I just want to say something to you." She stopped talking and slowly looked up from the map, feeling the blood drain from her face.

"Yes?" she said calmly, clearing her throat.

"Um . . . I just want you to know . . ." Ken began, suddenly looking shyly at the ground and kicking a rock with his foot, "how much I respect you and value your friendship."

Elizabeth looked up. She saw Ken's soft blue eyes gazing down at her. Her stomach relaxed.

"I really care about you, too," she said, not knowing what to say. Ken took a deep breath and hooked his thumbs in his back belt loops.

"I mean, you've really kept your head out here, despite every possible danger and setback," Ken managed to get out.

"I think everyone's done a pretty good job of handling the situation," Elizabeth said, shrugging slightly. Her heart was pounding.

"Yeah, but you've got your feet on the ground, Liz," Ken said, watching a wren land in the dry grass. "I don't know what I'd do if you weren't out there somewhere in the world. I'd never want anything to happen to you."

Elizabeth couldn't believe what she was hearing. Their eyes locked in a single moment of understanding that seemed to span a lifetime. They were standing in comfortable silence, only inches apart. She wanted to throw her arms around Ken. Then Elizabeth saw a vision of Todd's warm, coffee-colored eyes.

91

"Thanks," she said. She smiled warmly at Ken as she slung on her backpack. "Now, we've got a long way to go. And we don't know what may be out there."

"I thought you said we'd be winding back down to the riverbed. We've been climbing steadily for over an hour," Bruce complained. *It's time for someone who knows what they're doing to step in and read the map,* he silently resolved.

"Have we?" Todd said vaguely. Bruce let out a long-suffering sigh. It was boring always having to deal with people so much less intelligent than he was.

"My senile great-grandmother can read a map better than you can," Bruce said. "Has it occurred to you that this little detour is no mere few hundred yards?"

"It's occurred to me," Todd answered.

This guy is such a loser it's unreal, Bruce thought. Why hadn't he stolen Elizabeth from Todd when he had the chance—just for the amusement of seeing the guy squirm?

"Brilliant, Einstein, so why don't you—" Bruce began. But then he stopped dead in his tracks. Why *were* they climbing higher and higher? And Todd had been hiking for the last hour with the enthusiasm of a military cadet.

Suddenly everything became sickeningly clear to Bruce. Todd had changed course to catch up with Elizabeth and Ken!

"You're busted, Wilkins," Bruce yelled up to

Todd. "You've done some creative map reading to track down Wakefield and Matthews. Hope you're not sorry about what you find when you get there."

"So what?" Todd demanded. He spun around, his eyes boring into Bruce. "It only took you an hour to figure it out. Are you expecting a prize?"

"You're so pathetic," Bruce said, laughing in disgust. "Elizabeth has you wrapped around her little finger, doesn't she?"

"Take a long walk off a short cliff," Todd yelled back as he stormed ahead. Bruce followed him until they stood face-to-face at the top of the mesa.

"Not bad, Wilkins, you had me fooled. Maybe the desert will shake the wimp out of you yet," Bruce said, catching his breath.

"Look, I don't care what you do or think," Todd said firmly. "But I'm going to find her." He turned on his heels and left Bruce standing alone on the mesa.

"Be sure to give her a kiss for me," Bruce called after him.

"At least I finally understand what's important," Todd yelled. "Unlike you. You're still clutching for dear life to that jinxed bag of gold."

"That rock face must be a hundred feet high," Elizabeth said, catching her breath. "What should we do?"

They had made good progress crossing over a wind-rippled sand dune. Elizabeth was glad the morning hike hadn't been too challenging. Every bone and muscle in her body was reaching a point of deep fatigue. A night's rest hadn't been enough to rejuvenate her, especially with so little food. Now they stood at the foot of a craggy mountain face.

"Looks like the only way to go is up," Ken observed.

"Looks like it," Elizabeth wearily agreed. She slumped down onto a rock.

Ken crouched next to her. "You OK, Liz?" he asked.

"I'm fine," Elizabeth answered, hearing the defeat in her voice. "I'm just so incredibly tired."

"I know," Ken said. His eyes were filled with concern. "Listen, how about if you rest a minute and I check out the best way for us to climb up?"

Elizabeth smiled gratefully. Ken touched her lightly under her chin with his index finger and walked off to look around. As Elizabeth looked up into the cloudless blue sky, a hawk circled overhead. *We're more likely to see Elvis Presley backpacking up this trail than rain and flash flooding today,* Elizabeth thought. *Maybe we should've taken the lower route. This way is probably no less dangerous.*

"I found a good place to start climbing," Ken called to Elizabeth as he walked back to where she was sitting.

"Are we going to need equipment?" Elizabeth asked, standing up.

Ken placed his hands on his hips and squinted up the side of the mountain. "I don't think so," he decided.

Elizabeth could see that there were a lot of

footholds in the rock. They wouldn't need to drive metal spikes into the mountain to have something to hold on to. They also wouldn't need ropes to pull themselves up or to fall back on. The less encumbered their hands were with unnecessary ropes and spikes, the faster they could reach the top.

"OK, let's go for it," Ken said, taking a deep breath. "Liz, why don't you go first?"

"You'll catch me if I fall, right?" Elizabeth joked, knowing that if she fell from that height Ken would have only two choices: be crushed by her, or step aside and let her go splat on the rocky ground.

"You won't fall," Ken said. The corners of his eyes crinkled with laughter.

"Let's hope not," Elizabeth said a silent prayer.

"You'll make it, Liz," Ken said in a more serious voice. "I know you will."

Elizabeth gripped the jutting rocks with her fingers and hoisted herself onto the first craggy step. After climbing about twenty feet she looked down, then squeezed her eyes shut at the height. Her stomach twisted with fear. She turned her gaze back to the rock face and pushed ahead.

Reaching for the rocks with one hand, then the other, Elizabeth stepped up into each firm foothold. Gradually, she found a rhythm in the climb. *Just keep moving and don't look down,* she told herself over and over. Hours seemed to pass.

When Elizabeth finally looked up, she saw that she'd nearly reached the top. Her heart raced with anticipation. *I'm almost there!* She extended her hand over the edge of the cliff, ready to pull herself past the last few feet to safety. But suddenly the shale shelf she was standing on gave way beneath her.

She gasped in shock and terror. *This can't really be happening!* Elizabeth scrambled desperately to regain her footing. But with each step the solid rock under her feet broke off into chunks and fell away.

"Ken!" Elizabeth screamed. But there was no reply. Elizabeth forced herself to look down. The sight of the sheer hundred-foot drop made her almost sick with dizziness. Ken was just a small dot in the distance. She hadn't realized how quickly she'd been climbing and how far above him she'd got.

Every rock Elizabeth tried to grab hold of with her free hand only crumbled beneath her palm. Even with the adrenaline rushing into her system, she was exhausted from hunger, thirst, and the relentless force of the pulsing sun. There was no way she could pull herself up. Out of the corner of her eye, Elizabeth saw two vultures circling above her. She shut her eyes tightly.

My life is over.

Chapter 8

Bruce sat down and admired the sprawling view of Death Valley from the top of the mesa. He patted his bag of gold. He'd been carrying it in his hand, unwilling to let it out of his sight.

He thought about how much he enjoyed being rich. He'd always been rich, of course, but not anywhere near what he was about to be. When he got home, he was going to buy a Jaguar for starters. He deserved it. Maybe his own jet. He was better off without Wilkins and his preachy remarks. Now he didn't have to worry about anyone else. *Just the way I like it,* he thought.

He shrugged out of his backpack, still clutching his gold, and lay down on the mesa, resting his free hand behind his head and looking up at the cloudless blue sky. He rolled over and pulled his journal out of his pack, along with the expensive fountain pen he'd brought. Bruce sat up, cradled his bag of gold in his lap, shook the fountain pen, and opened his journal.

Bruce's Journal Entry
Saturday Noon

This whole terrible trip is finally almost over. It's been an amazing catastrophe, except for the fact that I'll be returning to Sweet Valley colossally rich. And it'll finally be wealth that I can call my own. It bothers me that everything I have is really my dad's. I've never admitted that before.

I would never tell the other geeks on this trip that I'm writing all of this voluntarily. Especially Elizabeth. She'd flash one of those smiles of hers and gush about how I've finally discovered how much you learn about yourself when you write, which I couldn't care less about. Or she'd say that she was rubbing off on me, which is more stupider. Why am I wasting my valuable time writing about Elizabeth Wakefield, when I could be making a list of accessories to get for the Jaguar?

A piercing scream interrupted the silence, echoing off the walls of the mesa.

Was that a bat or a Wakefield? Bruce wondered with annoyance. He threw down his journal and grabbed his bag of gold. Then he scrambled to the edge of the mesa.

Bruce peered down and caught his breath at the sight of Elizabeth hanging by one hand to the crumbling cliff. Her frightened eyes pleaded up at him. Bruce was completely surprised by the swirl of his own emotions as he looked into her terrified face.

"Elizabeth!" Bruce yelled from above. "Give me your other hand!"

Elizabeth, her entire life passing before her eyes, vaguely heard someone calling her name.

What would happen to her mother and her father when they found out she had fallen from a rock face in Death Valley and died? And what would the school tell Mr. Collins, her favorite teacher and the faculty adviser of *The Oracle*? Mr. Collins had always counted on her and believed in her future as a writer.

It dawned on Elizabeth that now she had no future. She would never again have excited conversations about literature with Enid. She would never marry Todd and raise a family with him.

Todd! Where is he? Is he all right? Elizabeth's anger with him melted away in the hot sun beating down on her.

And her sister. *Is Jessica even alive?* As she grasped at the eroding precipice, Elizabeth wished more than anything to be back in her room on Calico Drive.

Then she felt a strong hand encircling her wrist. She was sure it must be an angel taking her to the next world. *I feel so tired, maybe I'm dead already,* she thought.

Elizabeth looked up toward the sun, which blocked out her view of the angel's face—a tall, dark, handsome angel. She saw the silhouette of his strong body and smiled up at him. At the same time, she saw a huge winged creature swooping in above his head. *That must be another angel,* she thought as she prepared to release her hold on the ledge.

"Elizabeth, you idiot! Do you *want* to die? Give me your hand!" Bruce yelled.

The familiar voice finally seeped into Elizabeth's brain. She squinted up into the sun and suddenly realized this wasn't the hand of an angel, but the paw of Bruce Patman. The flying creature above him flapped its great wings as it dived for a landing over Bruce.

Elizabeth realized with horror that it was a bald eagle. The eagle had a wingspan of over six feet and talons the size of meat hooks.

"Bruce!" Elizabeth screamed, coming to her senses. "We must be near her nest! She'll kill you!"

"I'm not worried about a stupid bird!" Bruce yelled back over the thunderous roar of the wings. "Just grab my hand!"

He could see he was going to need both hands to haul her up. Reluctantly, Bruce dropped his bag of gold onto the surface of the mesa. He felt for Elizabeth's fingers as they clawed at the rocks, and he clasped her hand.

"Easy does it, I've got you," Bruce shouted. Elizabeth nodded stiffly. She looked frozen with fear.

Just as Bruce was about to grab Elizabeth's forearm with his other hand, he stole a glance behind him. Right in front of his eyes, the eagle landed on top of his sack of gold.

Bruce's first instinct was to let go of Elizabeth and rescue his gold. The eagle might carry it off and drop it in the middle of the desert. Bruce grabbed the nearest stone he could reach and threw it at the eagle, hitting it squarely in the chest. But instead of scaring the bird away, the blow merely made it angry. The eagle flapped its powerful wings, let out a terrifying cry, and tightened its grip on the small canvas bag.

Bruce held Elizabeth with one hand and tried desperately to reach for the gold with the other, but it was a few feet too far away. He reached until his hand was inches from the sack. Then he felt Elizabeth's fingers slipping through his.

"Bruce!" Elizabeth screamed.

Still reaching for the gold, Bruce looked back into Elizabeth's clear blue eyes and felt something give deep within him.

"I've got you!" Bruce yelled, gripping her fingertips.

Without warning he had a flashing memory of kissing Elizabeth that night at her pool party. She'd been wearing only a bikini, and he remembered the feel of her back beneath his hands, the touch of her lips against his.

"I can't hold on any longer!" Elizabeth cried.

With a sudden surge of adrenaline Bruce grabbed

at Elizabeth's arms with both hands and pulled her safely onto the ledge. As she collapsed with exhaustion into his arms, Bruce watched the eagle take flight, his sack of precious gold clutched in the bird's talons.

Jessica and Heather sat on the ground of the campsite, their wrists bound with rope behind their backs. It was noon on Saturday and the sun glared directly overhead. Jessica's pack was lying at the edge of the campsite, its contents dumped out on the ground.

Dreamily, Jessica began to imagine that she was at home in Sweet Valley, standing in the Wakefields' large kitchen, scolding their dog, Prince Albert. A large, heavy hand gripped her shoulder, jarring her awake. With a start she looked up into the face of the convict gang leader.

"Wake up, princess," the man said, rubbing a hand over his rough, unshaven face. He winked at Jessica and Heather, then walked across the campsite, where he barked an order at one of the other convicts.

Jessica was exhausted. She'd barely fallen asleep the night before when the convicts had intruded on the girls' camp. The three men had spent the rest of the night going through every inch of Jessica's stuff, futilely searching for more gold.

"They're holding us hostage," Heather whispered.

Jessica glared at her. "At least I used my head and stayed quiet, waiting for those guys to leave," Jessica hissed. "You had to go and blow it by screaming like a lunatic."

"They would have taken us prisoner no matter what we did," Heather hissed back.

"Nothing is ever your fault, is it, Heather?" Jessica said, scowling at her. *She's trying to keep her cool,* Jessica thought, *but anybody can see that she's shaking like a leaf.*

Jessica was too hungry to be scared. In fact, she was starving. She slumped back, every muscle in her body aching. All she wanted to do was take a nap and console herself with dreams of Heather drowning in a vat of nail polish.

Jessica watched the convicts move around the campsite. They poked around in Jessica's stuff, which they'd already rooted through a thousand times. Two of them kept getting in each other's way.

"Why are you constantly underfoot?" the leader icily asked the other convict.

"I'm sorry, boss," the second convict said. "I only thought that—"

"Don't think. Do me that one favor," the leader said in a quiet, tense tone. He put one hand to his forehead, as if his partner had given him a tremendous headache.

If Jessica hadn't known her life was in mortal danger, she would've been amused by these clowns. The first one had straight black hair, cut in a bowl around his head. The second convict was almost bald, with just a fringe of fuzzy hair. They reminded her of two of the Three Stooges.

103

"We don't even know your names," Jessica observed cheerfully. "Mind if I call you Moe and Larry? You kind of remind me of them."

Moe turned around sharply like a cornered animal, his bowl haircut flaring out and flattening back onto his skull. He stared at Jessica with furious eyes.

"Not a single word out of you," he said meanly, pointing a warning finger at Jessica.

"You sure can take a joke," Jessica grumbled under her breath.

"Quiet!" Moe shouted. "Unless you wisely decide to tell us where you're hiding the rest of the gold."

"I've told you six thousand times, I don't know where the rest is," Jessica said.

"Then keep your mouth shut," Moe snapped. He stuck a boot up on a rock and opened a map across his thigh.

Jessica leaned her head back and studied the third convict. She hadn't heard him say a word. In fact, he seemed to stay apart from the other two. He was sort of nice looking, with dark curly hair and blue eyes. There wasn't anything weird enough about him to inspire a comic nickname. *I think I'll call him Jack,* she decided.

Jack seemed to notice Jessica watching him. Without altering his serious expression, he began to move toward her. When he put his hand in his back pocket, a shudder ran down her spine. *Is he reaching for a gun?* she wondered. The convict towered directly over Jessica, and she felt her pulse race when he knelt down beside her. *Please, if you're going to kill me, make it quick.*

"How're you two doing? Are you OK?" he asked softly.

"Thought you'd never ask," Heather said flirtatiously. Jessica would have kicked her if she could have reached that far.

"Do you need water?" he asked in a sincere voice.

Jessica nodded vigorously. "And one other thing. I have a granola bar in the side pocket of the blue pack. Could you get it for us, please?" she asked hopefully.

He nodded. A moment later he returned with two tin cups of water and the granola bar. Then he reached his hand into his back pocket again. Goosebumps tingled on Jessica's arms.

"Here, want some beef jerky?" he asked, pulling a hunk of it from his pocket. He tore it in half and fed the pieces to Jessica and Heather, along with the granola bar.

"Thanks," Jessica said, not daring to look away from him. She took a bite of the jerky, then of the granola bar, then took a big drink of water.

"So where are you guys headed?" Heather asked with her mouth full.

"In other words, where are you taking us?" Jessica asked. He shrugged and looked off into the distance.

"What's your name?" Jessica asked.

"Why do you need to know?" he responded bluntly. Obviously, he wasn't into small talk.

"If you won't tell us your name, can I just call you Jack?" Jessica asked.

"Fine," he answered gruffly, arching an eyebrow at Jessica. "Better than being named after the Three Stooges," he said, smiling slightly. Jessica smiled, too, and suddenly felt a strange sense of relief.

"Well, now, look what I found," Moe said, digging in Jessica's stuff. "A flare." He held it up like a prize.

Jessica frowned. That flare had been their last hope to alert anyone to disaster. But it dawned on Jessica that even if the convicts hadn't discovered the flare, she couldn't possibly use it. What good would it do to drag Elizabeth, Todd, Bruce, and Ken into this snake pit of a situation?

"Maybe we can sell it on a reservation," Larry said greedily.

"Nah, it's not worth that much. Maybe we should just set it off for fun," Moe answered, caressing the flare. "It's been a while since I've had the chance to play with explosives." *No, don't set it off,* Jessica begged silently.

"Go ahead, set it off. Then our friends will come back and rescue us," Heather said arrogantly.

"Maybe we'll just do that, little lady," Moe said, brightening up. "And I bet your friends have some gold we can get our hands on."

"Heather, you idiot," Jessica whispered harshly between clenched teeth. "Now you're going to get *all* of us killed."

Heather's eyes went wide with sudden comprehension. Then, with a toss of her head, she flipped her golden tresses over her shoulder and batted her eyelashes seductively at Larry. Jessica was nauseated

106

by Heather's melodrama, but she had to admit to herself—she *was* interested to see if feminine charms might get them out of this mess. Moe was looking Heather over. Jessica held her breath and waited to see what he would do.

"You have beautiful blue eyes," Moe observed, staring at Heather. "But don't even think of trying to manipulate me. It won't work, sweetheart. If there's any funny business, I can snuff you out like a candle anytime I want." He laughed a terrible, cruel laugh.

Too bad you've just met the one man in the world who can't be locked under your spell, Heather Mallone, Jessica thought ruefully. Jessica's momentary satisfaction was quickly replaced by a chill as she considered Moe's warning. It seemed terrifyingly possible to Jessica that no one in their camping group would make it out of the desert alive. *I have to do something—now!*

Jessica noticed that Larry was watching her with his arms folded across his chest. "Can I kill these two right now, boss? Just to get warmed up for the others?" he asked.

"No one is going to get killed," Jack said. He glared at Moe ready for a confrontation. Larry's face clouded over with disappointment.

"I thought we agreed I was in charge," Moe said pleasantly to Jack, his eyes gleaming.

"Boss, you *said* I could kill somebody," Larry whined to Moe. "It's been so long."

"Well," Moe said thoughtfully, still staring at Jack. "It all depends, doesn't it?" He suddenly held the flare up away from his body and set it off.

Jessica's heart leaped into her throat as she watched the dark orange-and-red smoke arc across the blue sky. Larry was staring at her, practically licking his chops, a violent glint playing in his eyes.

Any possible door of escape had just been slammed shut.

Chapter 9

"You saved my life, Bruce," Elizabeth said, closing her eyes and falling onto her back. She lay gasping, waiting for her heart to stop pounding.

"We almost lost you there," she heard Bruce say. Elizabeth opened her eyes to see him looking down at her with a worried expression on his face.

"I don't know how I can ever pay you back," Elizabeth said, still breathing hard.

"Oh, I'm sure we can come up with something," Bruce responded. They both laughed. The tension that had built up between them during this whole awful trip had suddenly dissolved within a few terrible seconds.

"I'm sorry you lost your gold," Elizabeth said.

"There's a lot of gold in the world," Bruce said with a shrug. "But not too many Wakefields—fortunately!"

"Hey, watch it, Patman!" Elizabeth cried, sitting

up and coming to life. She tried to give him a playful kick but didn't have the energy. Bruce placed a gentle hand on her shoulder to get her to lie back down.

"You can punch me out later. Right now just rest," he instructed her.

"You're a pain in the neck," Elizabeth said with affection.

"So are you, Liz," Bruce whispered.

Just then Elizabeth heard Todd's voice and sat up again.

"Patman, is that you?" Todd called up. His voice sounded tired and full of despair.

"Up here, Wilkins," Bruce yelled back.

"I backtracked Ken and Elizabeth's route, but I can't find them anywhere," Todd yelled irritably from the trail.

He went looking for me! Elizabeth's heart filled with a rush of love for Todd.

"They might be dead for all I know," Todd continued bitterly. "If I've lost her for good, I hope you're satis—"

Todd reached the top of the mesa. She watched the fatigue in his face turn to shock and then to joy.

Energy shot through her limbs as she jumped to her feet and threw herself into Todd's arms. They held each other tightly for a long moment. Finally Todd pulled back and took her face in his hands. He pressed his lips to hers in a deep kiss.

"I'm sorry for not sticking by you," he said. His brown eyes were warm with love. "And I'm sorry for being so stupid and full of pride about doing such a

110

bad job of reading the map. It really was my fault for not paying closer attention during training."

"I've already completely forgiven you," Elizabeth said quietly. "But thanks for telling me that."

Todd glanced over at Bruce, and the softness in his face turned to suspicion.

"Elizabeth better not be hurt, Patman," Todd said angrily. Elizabeth took a deep breath and looked at Bruce. Then she told Todd the whole story.

"If it weren't for Bruce, I wouldn't have made it," Elizabeth said, reaching over and giving Bruce's hand a squeeze.

"That's all the thanks I get for saving your life?" Bruce asked. "I should have chosen the gold." But Elizabeth knew he didn't mean it, and a moment of genuine warmth passed quietly between them.

"Well, is anybody hungry?" Todd asked, running a hand through his hair. "We still have one granola bar between us, don't we, Bruce?"

"Peanut butter chocolate chip," Bruce answered. Bruce pulled the bar out of his pack and broke it into thirds, handing one piece to Todd and one to Elizabeth.

"The desert is making a human being out of you, Patman," Todd observed wryly. Bruce shrugged and rubbed Elizabeth's shoulder with one hand.

"Look!" Todd suddenly shouted, pointing toward the horizon. Elizabeth and Bruce turned quickly. Elizabeth's heart was in her mouth as she watched a faint plume of dark red-and-orange smoke rising into the clear sky.

"It's Jessica!" Elizabeth cried. "She's in trouble!" Every possible emergency ran through her mind. The two girls could be sick from drinking unpurified water. Or under attack by a band of mountain lions— or worse. Elizabeth brought her hand to her mouth, remembering Heather's insistence that there were three escaped convicts pursuing them on the desert trail.

"It's always *something* with you Wakefields," Bruce said, watching the smoke and shaking his head.

"I wish this were simply one more normal episode in the Wakefield Sisters' Circus," Elizabeth said with a growing sense of alarm. "But I have a feeling this is real trouble. Come on, let's go."

Just then they heard another voice from somewhere far below.

"What's going on up there?" Ken called.

"Ken!" Elizabeth exclaimed. "I almost forgot! He must be wondering where I am."

"Well, he probably figures you haven't fallen," Bruce observed. "Or he would have seen you plummet past him on the way down to the bottom."

"True enough," Elizabeth said, walking to the edge of the cliff to call down to Ken. She peered over the side of the rock, but reeled at the height and stepped back.

"Now that we've found Ken, we have to agree not to separate from each other again," Todd said firmly.

"I don't know if that's the safest strategy," Elizabeth said. She looked into the distance at the swirling smoke of the flare. *Jessica and Heather are*

112

in some kind of jeopardy, but what kind, exactly? she asked herself. "What if there's a trap?" Elizabeth wondered aloud.

"All the more reason to stick together," Todd insisted. "We've got strength in numbers."

Elizabeth didn't want to have any more fights with Todd on this trip. But something told her that she couldn't agree with him on this one.

"No, I really don't think we should approach the camp together," Elizabeth said. "Who knows what we'll find?"

"OK," Todd said, nodding his head slowly. He was obviously taking her hunch seriously. "What do you want to do, Liz?"

"Tell Ken to climb back down and follow behind us," Elizabeth decided. "We'll meet up again at Jessica and Heather's campsite."

"I love a good party," Moe said, rubbing his palms together. "Can't wait to meet your friends."

At Moe's instructions Larry hoisted Jessica and Heather to their feet, leaving their wrists tied.

"You two girls should stand over here in this clearing, if you please," Moe said with phony graciousness, gesturing at a patch of grass between two saguaro cacti. "You'll be perfect bait for your companions. They ought to be running bravely to your rescue any minute now."

"And don't try to run for it—we've got you covered," Larry said, drawing a gun from his pocket.

"Not a bad idea," Moe said, pulling out his own

weapon. He aimed the gun straight at Jessica and cocked the trigger. Jessica's stomach dropped to her shoes. As she drew a sharp breath, she noticed Jack crouching nearby, watching Larry and Moe with a look that she read as pure disgust.

"Knock it off, you guys, and put away the guns," Jack said, standing up. "What are they going to do, bolt into the nearest drugstore and call the cops?"

"You know," Moe said to Jack, running an affectionate finger along the barrel of his pistol, "I'm just not seeing the kind of enthusiasm and team spirit from you that I usually like to see in people running from the law with me."

"I'll be sure to work on my cheerful good-neighbor attitude for you," Jack said dully. "Remember that we're in this only for the gold. If you get your kicks by hurting a few nice people, don't do it on my time. I don't plan to go back to the pen."

"Funny, I don't believe I asked for your opinion about our agenda," Moe said calmly.

I can't stand to listen to any more of this! Jessica thought wildly. She was terrified to imagine what would happen when Elizabeth, Bruce, Todd, and Ken got there. Jessica figured they'd be lucky if the convicts took the remaining bags of gold and then left them tied up to mummify in the scorching sun.

But then an even more horrible thought flashed through her mind. *They'll probably take the gold and murder us all on the spot.* Jack said nobody would get killed. But why should Jessica trust him? *Even if he does have soft blue eyes.*

114

Jessica watched Jack lean down and run his fingers across a row of orange poppies. He *seemed* different from the other two, but how did she know he really was? *He's still an escaped convict,* she reminded herself. *He probably gunned down an entire fast-food restaurant just for kicks.*

Jessica realized with a stabbing pain in her chest that this was it. She was going to die. And the last person she was going to see was Heather Mallone. They'd better not end up on the same afterlife cheerleading squad!

"Any way you slice it, we'll be vulture food," Jessica said grimly to Heather. "Thanks to you."

"Well, at least we won't have to die out here alone." Heather glared at Jessica. "Ken and Bruce will die with us."

"Heather, since we're sharing our last moments on the planet together, I've always wanted you to know how pathetic I think your self-centeredness is," Jessica said, shaking her head in disbelief.

"Look who's talking," Heather responded in a cool, even tone. "You're not exactly Mother Theresa."

Though Jessica would never let it show, Heather's contemptuous comment seared her. She suddenly saw her life clearly. She was about to die, and what would she leave behind but a few cheerleading successes? Even Heather had that much. Jessica realized that all her life her main concern had been Jessica, whereas her sister had always thought of others. But now things were different—all Jessica could think about now was how to keep her beloved twin out of this mess.

Her thoughts were interrupted by the sight of three people walking down the trail leading to the campsite. Jessica felt her knees go weak with panic. She and Elizabeth had always shared a strong psychic connection. Jessica concentrated with everything in her power to send a message to her twin. *Elizabeth, stay away. For your sake, please just stay away!*

"Liz, slow down, you'll exhaust yourself," Todd said. "We'll get there, don't worry."

"How can I not worry? Besides, I'm fine," Elizabeth said, completely winded. She bent down and pulled spiky cholla-cactus balls off her socks. Her mouth was parched, but she didn't care. All she wanted was to reach her sister before . . . before what? *I can't think about that now. What if we're too late already?*

"There they are, way up ahead," Bruce called. Elizabeth squinted in the direction he was pointing. Jessica and Heather were standing in a clearing, and they looked perfectly safe!

"I'd say that neither of them are looking their high-fashion best," Todd commented. "But they're definitely alive."

"Elizabeth, you look like a cat that's been chased up a tree," Bruce noted. "Relax, they look fine." Elizabeth stood with a hand on one hip. She used her other hand to shade her eyes.

"They do look like they're just hanging around," Elizabeth concurred. "They're not exactly fighting off a fierce band of desert tortoises."

"If this is one of Jessica's little tricks, so help me—" Bruce said loudly. Elizabeth instinctively put a finger to her lips.

"We should make as little noise as possible as we move closer to the camp," she said.

"Like, no howling?" Bruce said in a loud whisper.

"This is serious," Elizabeth retorted, jabbing him lightly in the ribs.

"They see us," Bruce said as he, Elizabeth, and Todd crested the hill just a short way from the campsite. Despite her own intuition to be cautious, Elizabeth was so energized to see Jessica breathing and in one piece that she broke into a light sprint toward the grassy clearing, with Bruce and Todd behind her.

"We saw the flare," Elizabeth said, catching her breath. Jessica nodded soberly. Elizabeth had expected Jessica to leap happily into her arms. *Why is she just standing there?* she wondered.

"Whatever happened, we're here now. Everything's going to be OK," Todd said reassuringly.

Elizabeth saw that even in this heat Jessica's and Heather's serious faces were deadly pale.

"I've got a great idea," Bruce said, looking around the site nervously, disconcerted by the two girls' strange behavior. "Let's pack up your stuff and get out of here."

"Come on, Jess, we're almost home," Elizabeth said, squeezing Jessica's shoulder. But Jessica just pursed her lips and firmly gestured her head toward the trail.

117

"What in the world is the matter with you, Jess? Why are you making those strange faces?" Elizabeth asked, puzzled by Jessica's obstinacy.

Then she saw that Jessica's hands were tied behind her back. Elizabeth froze in her tracks. "Why—" she began uncomprehendingly.

Suddenly, three men in blue jumpsuits surrounded the entire group, staring with hard, vicious eyes. Elizabeth's heart skipped a beat as she found herself staring down the barrel of a gun.

Chapter 10

"You must be the three men we heard about on the news," Elizabeth said, staring at the armed strangers. "The ones who escaped from . . . prison." The last word died in her throat as she caught sight of Heather's terrified eyes.

"We've got a smart one here, don't we?" Moe said, chuckling.

"We sure do, boss," Larry said with a crooked grin. Moe glared at Larry, who dropped his goofy expression and shuffled his feet on the ground.

"As I was saying, we're so pleased to have you all here," Moe said, strolling around the campsite. "It was very nice of you to accommodate us by providing a flare we could use to call this little meeting."

Elizabeth's mind was racing. She glanced wildly around for anything they could grab to fight their way out. *Maybe we could swing a cactus at the convicts,* Elizabeth thought. But she immediately dismissed the idea. How could they possibly use cacti to over-power three men with guns?

"If you've hurt them in any way . . ." Todd began. Elizabeth saw a hard glint in Larry's eye.

"Do we look like the kind of guys who would hurt anyone?" Moe asked with fake innocence.

That's exactly the kind of guys you look like, Elizabeth thought.

"Just tell us what you want and get it over with," Todd said, taking a step toward them.

"Good, good—someone practical who's ready to talk business." Moe smiled broadly. "All right, then, we'll make this conference nice and short."

"The shorter the better," Todd said, narrowing his eyes.

"Fair enough." Moe seated himself on a flat rock. "Some folklore was passed around prison that there was gold stashed in the caves out here in Death Valley. Unfortunately, your group has been foolish enough to get to it first. So hand it over." He stopped smiling.

"And make it fast," Larry added.

Elizabeth closed her eyes and wished she could go back in time. The gold had been nothing but a curse to them from the moment they'd found it. She thought with a shiver of the eagle's great talons as they sank like sharp teeth into Bruce's sack of gold and carried it away.

"I know we can't fight this," Bruce suddenly said. He threw down his pack with a dramatic gesture. "If you want my gold, you can have it. You just have to get it out of my pack yourselves. I'm too exhausted to go digging for it."

Elizabeth tried to keep the shock from registering on her face. What on earth was Bruce up to?

She caught Bruce's eye. He raised an eyebrow. *Is he actually crazy enough to try to bluff the convicts?* she wondered with amazement.

"Go get the gold out of his pack." Moe gestured to Larry, not taking his eyes from Bruce. Larry began rummaging in Bruce's pack while Moe stood guard. Elizabeth knew that in one second Larry would realize Bruce didn't have any gold, and they'd all be sunk. *They'll be so angry, they'll kill us on the spot,* she thought with a sinking heart.

"Watch out!" Bruce yelled. "A bobcat!"

Moe twisted sharply around to look. As soon as he turned, Bruce jumped on Larry, who was still bent over Bruce's pack, and tried to pull the gun away from him. Moe quickly saw what was going on and struck Bruce across the jaw with the butt of his pistol, knocking him to the ground.

"Bruce! Are you all right?" Elizabeth cried, springing over to him. He rolled from side to side, cradling his jaw in one hand.

"You think you're tough," Todd said angrily. "You're not so tough, terrorizing innocent people."

Larry pointed his gun straight at Todd's head.

"*No!*" Elizabeth screamed. Larry cocked the release.

Then Moe began to laugh lightly again.

"Not yet, my friend. Put it away," Moe said, waving off Larry, who slowly lowered his weapon. Moe eyed Todd, and his amused chuckle turned into vicious laughter.

"Stop, please, that's enough," Elizabeth finally said. The only thing left to do was to cooperate with the men. It was their only chance for survival.

"You can have the gold, all of it." Elizabeth set down her pack and pulled out her bag of gold. She dutifully handed it over to Moe.

"Now we're talking," Moe said magnanimously.

"Are you sure that's all there is?" Larry asked suspiciously.

"That's it," Elizabeth said firmly. "Now, will you please let us go? There's obviously nothing we can do to you."

Moe only smiled. "Oh, we can't let you go yet, little sister. Not when we're all just getting to know each other."

"I say we off 'em, boss—we've got the treasure," Larry said, ripping open the bag and digging his fingers into the yellow stones.

Elizabeth looked with fright at Todd, who gazed helplessly back at her. Then she remembered something. This really wasn't all of their gold. Ken still had a sack of it. Elizabeth wished she could signal him in some way. *What will happen when Ken finally reaches the campsite?*

Jessica had been watching Bruce's and Todd's displays of heroism with fear and disgust. Trust Bruce to try to be the hero at a time like this, and Todd to start spouting law and order like a cop on TV. What would Ken do if he were here?

She felt a wave of longing for her boyfriend. *What if Ken fell off a cliff, broke his leg, and died of heat exposure? What if I never see him again?* It seemed ridiculous that she'd ever been angry at him.

Jessica knew she shouldn't have been so stubborn with Ken about his strategy for crossing that river. He'd placed her at the end of the human chain only because she was physically strong—not because he didn't want to be near her. And he'd volunteered to stay at the campsite with Heather only because she was a dimwit show-off with a busted ankle who couldn't defend herself in the desert against a ground squirrel.

Jessica's heart constricted with love and pain as she thought of Ken's loyalty. *How could I ever have doubted him?* she asked herself now.

Just as Jessica brushed a hot tear from her face, she heard a light rustle in the high grass a few feet away. She turned swiftly in the direction of the sound. Ken stared back at her. At the sight of his gorgeous face, she felt every cell in her body light up. She struggled to get to her feet.

Ken put a finger to his lips and gestured for Jessica to look to her right. Jessica saw that Larry was sitting on a rock nearby, stamping out a cigarette with his foot. His gun lay on the ground beside him.

"Where do you think you're going, princess?" Larry demanded, grabbing his gun.

"Uh . . . nowhere," she stammered. "I just

needed to stand up and stretch, that's all."

"Well, keep your stretching confined to the six square inches you're standing on, got it?" Larry's eyes lingered appreciatively on Jessica for a long moment.

Despite Jessica's revulsion, the man's leer had suddenly given her an idea. Larry was obviously attracted to her. If she could distract him, maybe Ken could sneak up and grab his gun.

Jessica gave Ken a smoldering look. Still wearing the same sensuous expression, she turned to face Larry, who was still busy snuffing out his cigarette. Then she slyly arched an eyebrow back at Ken. He gave her a thumbs-up sign through the dry stalks of grass. Now it was up to her: Jessica Wakefield, sexy seductress of Sweet Valley High, was about to swing into action.

"Larry," Jessica said, batting her eyelashes, "my wrists hurt. Could you loosen the ropes just a teeny, tiny bit?" She inhaled voluptuously and did her best to look irresistibly vulnerable.

"You can manage just like you are," Larry answered, remaining fixed on his rock, eyeing her. Jessica struck an attractive pose and flashed a beautiful smile.

"I know this may sound strange, but there's something about you I really like," Jessica said with as much sincerity as she could dredge up.

"Baloney," Larry said cynically. But Jessica saw his ears redden. She was getting to him!

"I really think that deep down, you must be a decent guy," Jessica continued.

"Yeah, maybe," Larry said, shrugging and studying the ground.

"I'd really appreciate it if you could loosen the ropes a little. Then we could just sit and get to know each other," Jessica purred. Larry kicked a small tumbleweed with his foot but didn't respond. Jessica was getting worried. She didn't know exactly what to say or do next.

Finally he put down his gun and began walking slowly toward her. She smiled warmly, careful not to give away her immense relief. Larry bent over her to loosen the ropes, and Jessica and Ken locked gazes for an instant. She felt Larry's breath on her shoulder.

Ken leaped from the grass and dived for Larry's gun, closing his hand around the pistol. Larry dived for Ken, but Ken kicked him in the stomach. Larry rolled away, moaning. Just then, Moe appeared from nowhere and stomped on Ken's wrist. Ken cried out in pain and released the gun.

"Another one, huh?" Moe said with irritation. "We're going to make you pay for that, golden boy. Now, hand over your treasure."

Jessica's pulse raced as Ken handed Moe his sack of gold.

"That's a good boy," Moe whispered. Then he trained his pistol on Ken and cocked the trigger. Jessica felt a wave of nausea and thought she was going to faint.

Out of the wide desert sky came a clap of thunder and a bolt of lightning. Jessica nearly jumped out of her skin. Larry jerked at the crashing noise and his gun fired a single, piercing shot.

Jessica screamed, squeezing her eyes shut. Would she open them to find Ken lying in a pool of blood? Terror-stricken, she shivered and forced herself to open her eyes.

The ice around her heart melted as she saw that the bullet had missed Ken. He stood unharmed, lifting his face to the sky as it began to rain.

"This is the torrential downpour we were warned about," Elizabeth said, squeezing Todd's arm as water gushed from the sky. "That storm Thursday night was just for starters."

"The desert will turn into a flood zone in a matter of minutes," Todd yelled above the deafening roar of tons of water colliding with the hard-packed ground. Elizabeth could feel the weight of her already soaked and clinging clothing.

"We're safe on this rise, at least for a while," Elizabeth said.

A bolt of lightning streaked across the sky, and Elizabeth was suddenly energized by an idea.

The lightning! Elizabeth remembered something she'd read in the back pages of the survival training course manual. "We're going to get struck if we stay up here. We should get to lower ground, where it's safe." Then Elizabeth held her breath, waiting to see if her plan would work.

Moe's face lit up. "You'll all make lovely lightning rods," he said, taking the bait.

They'll leave us here and we'll be rid of them for

good. Elizabeth crossed her fingers in the pockets of her shorts.

"I'll tie them all together, OK, boss?" Larry said excitedly.

"For once you have an excellent idea," Moe said, standing in the driving rain with his hands on his hips.

Larry pushed Elizabeth against Jessica and Todd and roped them all together. Then he roughly pulled Bruce, Ken, and Heather into the cluster and tied them to the others.

"I'm happy to shoot the first person who attempts resistance," Moe said, aiming his gun.

Elizabeth saw the horror in Jessica's face, which was inches from hers.

"Try to relax," Elizabeth said to her twin through the pelting rain. "We'll be OK." Elizabeth hoped she could keep believing that herself.

The ropes tightened around Elizabeth's chest and burned into her wrists. She hoped she'd done the right thing by giving Moe the idea of leaving them on the butte in the lightning storm. Once the convicts left, they would have to untangle themselves quickly and get off the mesa. What if they were unable to loosen the tight knots in time?

"You can't just leave them here to die," a voice suddenly boomed.

"Jack!" Jessica whispered.

"Who?" Elizabeth asked. But no sooner had she spoken than the third convict strode angrily toward Moe. He'd stood on the sidelines since Elizabeth had arrived with Bruce and Todd, leaving most of the talking to the others. Why did he even care what happened to them? *I hope he doesn't stop Moe from leaving us behind on the mesa,* Elizabeth prayed.

"Be a nice boy and lend a hand so we can get out of here fast, got it?" Moe spat at Jack, who only glowered furiously back at him.

"Why is he doing this?" Elizabeth asked Jessica over the roar of the rain.

"I don't know," Jessica said. "But that guy, Jack, isn't all bad. He gave me water and beef jerky before when Moe wasn't looking."

Elizabeth gazed at Jack, who was still yelling ferociously at Moe. *I don't understand why Jack's helping us, but I'm glad he's here,* she decided. Jack finally threw up his hands in resignation and stormed off to the edge of the campsite. Elizabeth's stomach quivered. Moe and Jack had very nearly had a fatal showdown over the fate of the group!

"Let's get down where we're safe," Moe yelled when he had made sure all the ropes were tight. He and Larry grabbed their knapsacks and took off down the hillside. Jack followed them, but stopped for a moment to look sadly back at the six young people bound together in the rain. Then he disappeared down the trail.

Chapter 11

"They're gone!" Jessica whooped. "We're free!"

"That was too close for comfort," Todd said, with a great, exhausted sigh.

"I've never been so relieved in my life," Elizabeth said, relishing the feel of the rain as it cleansed her face and hair. She was exhilarated by the simple sensation of life coursing through her.

"We're so incredibly lucky," Heather said, taking a deep breath.

"Luck nothing, we're the toughest group of hikers SVSS has ever sent into the desert," Ken yelled.

"Let's hear a big round of applause for us!" Jessica hollered in return.

Everyone laughed helplessly, including Elizabeth. Somehow the idea of clapping—when all of their arms were tightly bound—struck her as the funniest thing she'd ever heard. The group's laughter relaxed and warmed Elizabeth, despite the chill of the rain.

"Listen, it's terrific that we could all get together like this," Bruce said. "But let's untangle these ropes and get out of here.

"Sounds good to me," Ken agreed.

A bolt of lightning flashed through the sky, followed a second later by a clap of thunder. "We have to hurry and get out of this exposed area," Elizabeth said. "I was telling the truth—we really are in danger of being struck up here."

"Right," Todd said, starting to work at untying the ropes. Cooperating like gears in a clock, the whole group began to untangle themselves from Larry and Moe's complicated knots.

"Nice work, Jessica. It's good to see you too busy to complain about anything," Bruce said.

"You owe me for that one, Patman," Jessica said cheerfully as she began to slip out of her ropes.

Bruce finally freed himself and pulled a huge hunting knife from his pack. Then he cut the ropes that bound Todd's hands, while Todd stared at the enormous knife.

"What did you expect to do with that out here, skin bears?" Todd asked, smiling at Bruce.

"Something like that," Bruce said, grinning back.

"Is everyone ready to start hiking?" Elizabeth asked with urgency.

"Where do you expect to go? The trail is totally washed out," Jessica said, pushing strings of soggy hair out of her face.

Elizabeth looked down toward the trail and realized with horror that Jessica was right. The narrow

130

canyon below them had been deluged, sealing off the lower route. Elizabeth felt a strange tightening in her chest. Would the torrential rain cause a flash flood?

"We'll have to head up into the higher bluffs," Todd observed.

"The trails up there are really narrow, with a sheer drop off the cliff," Ken pointed out.

"There's no other choice," Todd said.

Elizabeth felt chilled once again as she gazed up toward the rocky bluffs. If Bruce hadn't saved her, she would have fallen from that cliff to her death. But the raging waters below were deepening. The river was going to flood! She hesitated as she stared up at the jagged rocks. But she knew she had to conquer her fear.

"Let's go!" Elizabeth called. She began scrambling up the rocks, leading the way for everyone. A bolt of lightning struck a stunted tree in a clearing less than half a football field away.

Suddenly Elizabeth heard a man scream from the swirling river. She turned abruptly in the direction of the scream. The pouring rain nearly blocked her vision. But it was late afternoon, and there was still enough light to see who was crying out.

"It's Jack!" Jessica shouted. "He's being carried away by the flood."

"We can't let him drown," Elizabeth yelled through the driving rain.

"If we try to save him, we'll all die," Bruce yelled.

"We can't just leave him here!" Jessica shrieked.

"We can fish him out with some of the longer

driftwood," Elizabeth suggested, jumping from the rocks and climbing down toward the ferocious waters. "He's close enough to the bank."

"Hang on, Jack, we're coming for you," Jessica sang out.

Heather limped to the edge of the mesa and climbed carefully down the jagged boulders to the river's edge. She stepped toward Elizabeth, then fell back onto the muddy rocks. "My ankle hurts. I can't help get him out," she called.

"Then stay where you are, Heather. We can't risk your falling in, too!" Ken yelled.

Elizabeth climbed down closer to the river, grabbing the shale as her feet slipped. She felt a strong hand take her arm firmly, steadying her. Elizabeth looked up to see Todd. He held her for an instant, pressing his lips warmly to hers.

Then he let go of her and leaped across the rocks. He grabbed a thick stalk of desert brush out of the crashing river.

"I can almost reach him," Todd called out.

Elizabeth saw that the river was heading toward a sheer drop. Jack was hurtling toward the edge of a hundred-foot waterfall.

"Todd, I'll help," Elizabeth called. She climbed quickly over the slippery rocks and stepped waist-deep into the river. Jack grabbed the stalk of brush that Todd held out. When Jack got close enough to the edge of the river, Elizabeth clasped his forearm. Jack clutched Elizabeth and she nearly lost her footing.

"I've got you, Elizabeth," Bruce called. He jumped down over the wet, mossy rocks and stepped into the wild river. Bruce put his arms around Elizabeth's waist. She leaned back against him as she held on to Jack's arm.

"Just don't let go, Bruce," Elizabeth said, clenching her teeth. It was taking all her strength to keep from slipping into the torrent of water under Jack's weight.

"I won't," Bruce promised into her ear.

With a final pull they hauled Jack to safety. He slumped across a rock, coughing water from his lungs.

Elizabeth stepped up onto the boulders a few feet above the riverbank. Buckets of rain continued to pour down. She watched Ken help Bruce and Todd climb out of the water, then Todd lean with exhaustion against the rocks and close his eyes.

Elizabeth, drained and weary, was vaguely aware of water lapping over her shoes. Suddenly alarm shot through her limbs as she realized that the thrashing river was rapidly rising.

"We don't have any time to spare," Elizabeth yelled, springing to life. "If we stay here, we'll drown!"

She scrambled up the rocks. Todd and Bruce followed her, with Jessica and Ken close behind. Elizabeth glanced far below and caught sight of Heather gingerly stepping across the treacherous rocks as the river licked at her feet.

What if Heather couldn't keep up with them as the river rose higher and higher?

"Wait, I can't go that fast!" Heather suddenly shrieked. "Don't *leave* me here!"

"How are we going to get her up?" Elizabeth yelled down to Todd, feeling rising panic.

"I don't know. None of us are strong enough to carry her straight up like this," Todd responded.

Elizabeth was terrified. She looked down at Heather's face, which even at a distance was clearly contorted with agony. If they didn't move fast, they would all be washed into the pounding river and dashed on the rocks.

"Help me, *please!*" Heather sobbed in pain as a wave crashed up to her shoulders.

"Just *try* to climb up," Elizabeth pleaded.

Bruce gripped the rocks and pulled himself onto the mesa. Ken, Todd, and Elizabeth climbed over the edge. They clasped Jessica's hands and pulled her to safety.

Elizabeth looked down and saw the river thrash over Heather's head. The water tore her hands from the rocky shelf. Heather screamed and vanished from sight. Elizabeth stopped breathing.

Just then Jack climbed up from the ledge below. He had Heather in his arms! He lifted her onto his shoulder and carried her up the rocks as the river ripped into the jagged cliff. Elizabeth saw the clear outline of muscles beneath his drenched jumpsuit.

"They'll never make it," Bruce said with frustration. "They'll make it," Elizabeth insisted, breathing hard.

The river pounded against the struggling pair as

Heather clung tightly to Jack. Finally his large hands reached the mesa.

"Help me get them over the edge," Todd yelled. He gripped Jack's muscular forearm.

But the shale crumbled beneath Jack's hands. His eyes opened wide with terror.

"He's slipping!" Elizabeth shrieked.

"Heather's weight is too much!" Todd yelled.

Bruce quickly reached for Heather. "Heather, put your arms around me," he commanded.

Heather stretched her arms up to Bruce. He pulled her against his chest, and she wrapped her arms around him. He carried her onto the mesa as Jack hoisted himself over the edge.

"It's OK," Bruce said quietly, cradling her head in his hand. Heather sobbed as he held her tightly.

They all found shelter together under a large out-cropping of rock, at a safe distance from the river. Bruce gently laid Heather on the ground. He ran his hand across her forehead, smoothing her wet hair away from her eyes.

Jack collapsed onto his back, breathing heavily.

Elizabeth gazed at Jack. *Whoever he really is, he's part of us for now,* she thought.

"Jack," Elizabeth whispered hoarsely. "Welcome."

"I can't believe you saved my life," Jack said, leaning back against the rocks and watching the rain fall. "No one's ever done anything like that for me before."

"No one's ever saved me from drowning before,

either," Heather said. Bruce sat down next to her.

"Or stood up for me when an armed buddy insisted on leaving me to die," Elizabeth said, dropping her pack to the ground. She sat under the outcropping next to Todd.

"Yeah, some buddy," Jack said, looking down at the rocks beneath them.

Jessica sat down and leaned against the rock wall.

"Mind if I join you?" Ken asked, looking down at her.

"Have a seat," Jessica answered. She smiled and patted the ground next to her. Ken flopped down and put his arm around Jessica.

Jessica wondered what had happened in Jack's past that had forced him to turn to a life of crime. He looked so dignified—even imposing—gazing thoughtfully at them all beneath his shock of dark hair. She was vaguely conscious of Ken squeezing her shoulder. *I must look good in a desolate, windblown, rain-washed sort of way,* she thought absently. Jack had been a criminal, of course, but he'd probably decided to turn over a new leaf. To Jessica, it all sounded incredibly romantic.

"I have to apologize for those guys," Jack said. "They're not too bright."

And now Jack's alone in the world, without even his fellow outlaws for friends. Jessica was intrigued. She wanted to ask him a million questions about himself.

But Heather's shrill voice interrupted her thoughts. "Where are you from? Where did you go to school?"

she suddenly piped up, batting her eyelashes at Jack.

"I grew up in a small town in northern California, near the Oregon border," Jack said politely.

"Do you miss it?" Heather asked.

"Yeah, I miss it," Jack said quietly, gazing at Heather's face with his soft blue eyes. His warm tone was certainly a contrast to the curt answers he'd given when he and Larry and Moe had first taken Jessica and Heather as prisoners.

"What's your real name?" Jessica asked.

"Mmmm, how about if we skip that one for now?" Jack said, laughing gently. "I'm on the run, you know."

"I hate to break up this chitchat. But did anyone else notice that the rain is still coming down in buckets?" Bruce asked.

"We'll have to wait here until the storm passes," Elizabeth responded, leaning her head on Todd's shoulder.

"Which could be any minute, out in the desert," Ken added.

"Everyone at home must be worried about us," Elizabeth said miserably.

"SVSS has probably sent out a search party by now," Ken said.

"Anybody worrying about you back home?" Todd asked Jack.

"Yeah," Jack answered with misty eyes.

"Got a girlfriend?" Heather asked, raising an eyebrow. Bruce nudged her in the ribs. Jessica glared at her.

Jack smiled and unzipped a side pocket in his jumpsuit. He pulled out a small sealed plastic bag and opened it. Inside was a photograph. He gazed lovingly at the picture and handed it to Jessica. Heather craned her neck to see.

"Wait your turn," Jessica said archly. She studied the photograph. "She's beautiful."

"Let me see," Elizabeth said, leaning toward Jessica. "What a pretty silver locket around her neck."

"I thought so. That's why I gave it to her," Jack said with a slight grin.

"When was the last time you saw her?" Ken asked.

"She visited me about six months ago," Jack said, shrugging. Jessica saw his eyes well with tears. "She writes to me a lot, though." He pulled out another plastic bag, which contained a stack of letters.

"Is she waiting for you to get out of prison?" Heather asked.

Jack nodded. "I'm going to send for her as soon as I get across the border." He ran his thumb gently along the edge of one of the envelopes.

"She must really love you," Elizabeth said quietly.

Jack smiled. Jessica noted that his smile was gorgeous.

"Hey," Jack said, looking through his knapsack. "I just remembered the brownies she baked for me." He pulled a small blue metal tin from his sack, then pried off the top. "Not even soggy. There's enough for each of us to have one."

"They even have walnuts!" Heather said.

"I'll take one of those off your hands," Bruce said. Jack passed around the tin and everyone dug into the brownies.

"This is the best thing of any kind I've ever eaten in my life," Ken said with his mouth full.

"I know what you mean," Elizabeth agreed.

"I wouldn't have had the strength to walk another ten yards without any food," Heather said, choosing a brownie from the tin.

"You read my mind, Heather," Todd said. He leaned against the rock wall and ate the fudge frosting off the side of his brownie. "Until this trip, I never knew what it was like to be severely hungry."

"Same here," Ken said.

"You know what would be great right now? A steaming platter of spaghetti and meatballs, with plenty of parmesan cheese," Jessica murmured. She leaned against Ken, who put his arms around her and kissed her softly on the neck.

"Wakefield, are you fantasizing about food?" Bruce asked.

"Come on, Bruce, what would you eat right now if you could have anything in the world?" Jessica teased.

"Oh, let me see. Anchovy paste on French crackers and garlic sautéed snails," Bruce answered, closing his eyes as if to savor the grotesque image.

"That's disgusting, Patman," Ken interjected. "Whatever happened to normal, boring things like hamburgers and hot dogs?"

"No, you guys, the best thing right now would be

a hot bowl of mushroom-barley soup," Elizabeth said, giving Todd a neck massage.

"And a chocolate shake with fries to go with it," Heather added. Elizabeth and Heather made faces at each other and then started laughing.

"Jack, how did you escape from prison?" Heather finally asked, licking chocolate from her fingers. Jack puffed out his cheeks and exhaled thoughtfully.

Jessica decided she'd show Jack that she could ask much more interesting questions than Heather. "I'd like to know what crime you committed in the first place," she said boldly. Elizabeth stared in horror at Jessica.

"No, no, it's all right," Jack said to Elizabeth shyly. He turned back to Jessica. "In fact, you have a right to know the answer." Jessica shot the glowering Heather a glance of victory.

"I was in for armed robbery," Jack explained. "A couple of guys talked me into holding up a liquor store with them. It got me a ten-year sentence."

"How much of the sentence did you serve?" Elizabeth asked.

"Three years. Then I decided to break out," Jack said. "Which brings me to your question," he said warmly to Heather, who beamed annoyingly.

"So how'd you do it?" Ken asked.

"Well, I got ahold of a map of all the prison's secret basement passageways. I paid off a guard to get me a copy of the security-watch schedules. My girlfriend sent me the money. Then, just as the coast was clear and I was ready to bolt with my knapsack of supplies, Moe appeared with his sidekick, Larry."

"That must have been fun," Jessica said.

"A barrel of laughs," Jack said dryly. *Well, he might be a thief,* Jessica thought, *but he's cute and smart and has my kind of sense of humor, not to mention more guts than any guy at Sweet Valley High.*

"Moe said he'd been watching me," Jack went on. "He said he knew I was a smart guy who would find a way to get us all out. Then he pulled a gun and suggested that I might enjoy some company." Jack paused, clenching his teeth at the memory.

"What did you do?" Todd asked.

"What could I do? Just as he pulled his weapon, all the lights went on and the alarm sounded. In the time I had wasted standing around with those two clowns, the guards discovered we'd got out of our cells," Jack said with a deep sigh. "I told those two to shut up and move fast. We made it outside the prison walls and down into a manhole just in time."

"But how did you get way out into Death Valley?" Bruce asked. He shifted his weight and leaned closer to Heather.

"Moe said there was gold hidden in the desert and that we should go get it—using my supplies," Jack explained. "I admit that I got caught up in the idea of finding gold and getting rich. But I didn't figure on the danger and trouble it would cause."

"What are you going to do now?" Elizabeth asked. Jack folded up his long legs and wrapped his arms around his knees.

"When I get across the border, I'm going to find a

way to go back to school and really make something of myself," Jack said with a faraway look in his eyes.

"Maybe if we explain to the authorities how brave and self-sacrificing you were for all of us, they'll forgive your escaping from prison and let you start a new life," Jessica said hopefully. She knew it wasn't too likely that Jack would be excused for making a prison break, as if he'd cut a few classes. But she really wished that he could get a second chance.

"You're a nice girl," Jack said, smiling sadly at Jessica. "I wish everyone was as nice as you."

"Or as nice as *you*," Elizabeth added. Jack shrugged and glanced gratefully at Elizabeth.

"Well, we all have one thing to be thankful for," Jack said, changing the subject. "We're lucky we got away from Moe alive."

"Why? What can you tell us about him?" Ken asked suspiciously.

"There's not much to say. Only that he's a cold-blooded killer," Jack said with a piercing look. "He's been convicted on the first-degree gun murders of five men and women. He also set off a series of explosions in residential urban areas, killing countless other people."

"Oh, no," Ken said quietly. Elizabeth covered her face with her hands. Jessica felt a chill, remembering how excited Moe had been about setting off the flare. But Moe couldn't possibly come after them again. He'd perished in the flood.

"Moe likes to toy with people, as you could all plainly see," Jack finally said. "But when he gets seriously angry, you don't want to be in the way."

"Well, he can't hurt us or anyone else now. Larry and Moe were washed away in that raging river," Jessica reminded everyone with a note of triumph. "We know that beyond a shadow of a doubt."

"This is one of the first times I've felt relaxed since this trip started," Elizabeth said. *Despite the fact that I'm sitting inches from an escaped convict,* she thought. She nestled closer to Todd under the outcropping.

"I know what you mean," Todd said, kissing the top of her wet head.

"Right," Heather added sarcastically. "We're sitting who knows where in Death Valley, in the middle of a flash flood. This is almost as relaxing as a week at Club Med."

Bruce laughed and glanced appreciatively at Heather. "I think this has Club Med topped by far," he said, giving Heather's shoulder a squeeze. Heather giggled. Elizabeth eyed the cozy pair, then tossed Todd a sideways look. Todd shrugged.

"Your jaw still looks bruised from when Moe hit you," Heather said to Bruce, running her hand down his cheek. Todd shot a sideways glance back to Elizabeth, who grinned.

"How did all of you end up in the desert? Did you come out here for a treasure hunt, too?" Jack asked.

"Can we talk about something more pleasant than the gold?" Bruce groaned. "Like nuclear war?"

"That bad, huh?" Jack said, the edges of his eyes crinkling in a smile.

"You don't know the half of it," Todd said.

Then everyone jumped in to tell Jack the story of how they'd all been taken by the idea of tracking down the gold and getting rich quick. Elizabeth noticed how Jack listened carefully as each person told his or her part of the story, occasionally nodding his head sympathetically. *He's really nice,* she thought. She wasn't ready to completely trust an armed bandit who was running from the law, but she was impressed by Jack's compassionate nature.

"That gold was bad news," Elizabeth said. "Now that we're rid of it, I finally feel safe." She sighed with relief. Then she noticed Jessica's forehead furrow in a guilty look.

"We *are* rid of the gold, aren't we, Jess?" Elizabeth asked, suddenly not wanting to know the answer.

"Almost," Jessica confessed in a barely audible voice.

"Almost?" Elizabeth inquired, her blood pressure rising. "Spill it, Jess. What's going on?"

"Well, when the rain started, Moe yanked the ropes off my hands so he could tie us all together. There were a few minutes of confusion. So I lifted Ken's gold from Moe's knapsack," Jessica explained.

"And you were planning to let that detail slip your mind, right?" Ken said, giving her a wry look.

"I was going to give it back to you!" Jessica said, defending herself.

Jack laughed along with the others. Elizabeth liked the sound of his laughter; it had a warm,

144

hearty resonance. She began to believe they might actually survive the trip together—all of them, including Jack.

"Here, it's all yours," Jessica said in a huff, fishing the gold out of her pack and tossing it into Ken's lap.

"Hey, don't give it to me," Ken laughed. He tossed it back to Jessica as if it were white-hot. "I don't want to have anything to do with it."

"Leave it behind, Jessica," Elizabeth advised. "Bury it next to a cactus when we hit the trail."

"*Bury* it? Are you crazy, Liz? Why bury a perfectly good bag of gold?" Jessica objected.

"Get rid of it, Jess," Elizabeth said in a firm tone of authority. "I have weird feelings about this gold. It's brought us only bad luck."

"We either need to build an ark or start walking," Jessica said. She stood and walked to the edge of the rock outcropping. The rain poured relentlessly.

"Jess is right," Ken agreed. "The rain's not letting up, and we only have a few more hours of daylight."

"Look at the bright side—at least we're not going to die of thirst," Jessica quipped, determined not to let the circumstances drag her down.

"We already know that the water will dry up within minutes after the rain stops," Elizabeth sighed.

"Then let's go fill our containers with falling rainwater right now," Jessica suggested.

The group followed Jessica out into the pouring

rain. They filled tin cups and heartily drank fresh rainwater.

Jessica was the first to put her pack on. She nudged everyone else to get ready to hike the final stretch. Then she strode back onto the trail, with the others following close behind. The seven of them, including Jack, all plodded on in the rain.

"Look at all the rabbits and lizards and pack rats running to their shelters," Heather said.

"I'm so hungry, I could grab one and eat it on the spot," Bruce said.

"You're a man of fine breeding, Patman," Todd yelled.

"Thanks, Wilkins, *I* thought so," Bruce answered, and they both laughed. *Everyone's doing great under my leadership,* Jessica thought.

An hour later the group stopped for a rest under a rock shelter.

"Do you want to take the lead again, Jess?" Elizabeth asked. "You've been doing a good job of keeping us hiking at a fast pace."

"No, you guys go on ahead," Jessica said. "I'll hang back a minute and find someplace to dump off the gold." Elizabeth gave Jessica a thumbs-up sign as she walked back to the trail.

Jessica knelt by a cactus and began digging a shallow hole in the hard ground. The rest of the group disappeared around a bend in the carved rock face. Jessica dropped the bag of gold into the hole and threw a handful of dirt over it.

But then she stopped. *Wait a second,* she thought.

Why is Elizabeth making all the rules, as if she were High Priestess of the Desert? From now on Liz should give her superstitious brain a rest and leave the practical decisions to me.

Jessica stuffed the bag of gold nuggets back into her pack.

Chapter 12

"I know Larry and Moe probably drowned in the flood," Elizabeth said. She adjusted the pack on her back and pulled the heavy windbreaker more tightly around her neck. "But I still feel uneasy."

"Let me guess," Bruce said, trudging through the wet sand. "You have a strange, uncomfortable sensation of being cold, tired, and hungry."

"I'm serious. I just have this funny sort of intuition, like there's danger lurking," Elizabeth insisted as she hiked. "I know it sounds crazy."

"No crazier than anything else about this insane camping trip," Bruce responded, zipping up his jacket. "I can't believe I ever thought it was romantic to walk on the beach in the rain."

"Bruce, I can't shake the feeling that the gold is actually cursed," Elizabeth continued. "Everyone who has tried to keep it has met with terrible disaster."

"I don't exactly call Larry and Moe meeting their

well-deserved end in the river a disaster," Bruce pointed out.

"They might disagree," Elizabeth replied. "Anyway, how about what happened to the travelers on the wagon train in 1849? The last diary entry said it was the pursuit of the gold that had torn them apart!"

"We don't even know what happened to them, Liz. All we saw was a pile of skeletons," Bruce said as they hiked past dripping mosses and small ferns.

"But what if the gold has cursed us, too?" Elizabeth asked, drawing a slow breath.

"Well, you don't have to worry about that anymore," Bruce assured her, his voice tinged with regret. "We managed to let all of it slip through our fingers."

"I guess you're right," Elizabeth reluctantly agreed.

The rain had caused every flower in the desert to open up. Elizabeth marveled at the carpets of white primrose and lilacs, all drinking with great thirst. She fell into a rhythm in her hiking. This slog through the unrelenting rain hardly even bothered her anymore. The cold, wet desert was beautiful, so alive with moisture and color. *We have nothing to worry about*, Elizabeth repeated to herself. *We're almost home.*

As the group rounded a bend near an outcropping of rock, Elizabeth felt almost lulled by the raindrops.

She heard a noise coming from a cave up ahead and felt a momentary twinge of fear. Then she saw a jackrabbit hop out of the cave, munching on wild grass. She relaxed and trudged past the dark entrance.

Suddenly Elizabeth gasped as someone grabbed her from behind! A strong arm clutched across her chest and a large hand flew over her mouth. She struggled for breath as she was quickly dragged into the cave.

"Elizabeth!" Todd yelled. He'd been walking right behind her. A flurry of bats that had been asleep in the cave were disturbed by the commotion and flapped noisily out. Ken's and Todd's arms flew up to protect their faces from the angry bats.

"Don't try to resist or you're dead," a deep voice hissed into Elizabeth's ear. *It's Moe!* Elizabeth thought wildly. *But how?*

"Let me go!" Elizabeth screamed, struggling to free herself from the man's grip.

Todd and Ken raced to the cave entrance and froze. Moe roughly pulled Elizabeth against him and pressed the cool blade of his knife to her throat.

"Don't kill her!" Heather screamed from behind Ken.

"OK, you jokers," Moe said. "One of you ripped off the gold from my knapsack. Hand it over, fast." Elizabeth cast a desperate look at Todd, pleading for him to do something. She saw the frightened, helpless look in his deep-brown eyes.

"Let her go," Todd demanded in a loud, frustrated voice. He walked into the cave. "We don't have the gold anymore. It's gone, the last of it was buried—" But before Todd could finish his sentence, Jessica stepped forward and opened her pack.

Elizabeth's whole body registered shock as she

saw the glint of gold peaking out of the top of the small canvas sack.

"Here, take it," Jessica said. She handed Moe the sack of gold.

Elizabeth's head was spinning. She tried not to faint as she felt the cold, sharp metal edge of the knife touching her skin. Jessica hadn't really got rid of the gold! Now its horrible curse was going to destroy them all.

Not only am I about to get my throat slit, I'm ready to kill Jessica for being such an idiot, she thought wildly. Elizabeth saw Jessica staring at her with pleading eyes. She glared back with a piercing gaze of red-hot anger. *Don't give me that lost-dog look this time!* her eyes said. Elizabeth was going to pound Jessica when—if—they got out of this.

"OK, you've got the gold. Now, leave us alone," Jessica said nervously. Ken took Jessica's hand and pulled her back to him. Elizabeth waited for Moe to release her. But he only tightened his grip and burst out laughing.

"I'm going to teach you a lesson about dealing with me," Moe said. He clutched Elizabeth and the bag of gold with one hand and held the knife to her throat with the other. Todd was staring at Elizabeth with wild disbelief.

Suddenly Larry appeared from the shadows, his eyes gleaming. He moved stealthily along the back wall of the cave.

"Please take your gold and let me go," Elizabeth

whispered to Moe. His face was less than half an inch from hers.

"Oh, I think you've run out of chances, sweetheart," Moe said. "Too bad you don't have nine lives, like me." He meowed menacingly in Elizabeth's ear, sending a shudder down her spine.

"We're sorry—my sister didn't mean to—" Elizabeth stuttered desperately.

"I'm sorry too, darlin'," Moe said mournfully. "It's just that nobody tries to pull one over on me and gets away with it. So shut up and prepare to die," he concluded with a harsh whisper.

"You've got what you want, so let her go!" Todd screamed. "This is cruel!" Bruce put a hand on Todd's arm.

"It *is* cruel, isn't it?" Moe whispered.

Elizabeth watched the bats flapping chaotically outside the cave. Jack had warned them that Moe was a ruthless killer who liked to play games, but who finished off his prey when the game was over. She closed her eyes in utter terror.

Maybe I do have nine lives, she thought in despair. *And the last of those lives is about to be spent.*

"Hold it right there. This has gone too far," Jack said, moving toward Moe in the cave. "Let her go, *Moe.*" Jack lingered sarcastically on the name Jessica had invented. Moe gave Jack a furious look. Jack began to move toward him very slowly.

"I wouldn't come any closer if I were you," Moe said, pulling his arm tighter around Elizabeth.

"Come on, knock it off," Jack said casually. But he stopped walking and stood quietly, placing a reassuring hand on Todd's shoulder. Jack knew it was essential that he keep a light, confident tone in his voice. Murderers could smell fear. If Jack sounded nervous, Moe might move in for the kill even faster. Jack knew Moe far too well, and he was taking the guy's threat against Elizabeth very seriously.

"*Jack.*" Moe suddenly laughed softly. "You look so *mad* at me. That hurts my *feelings.*"

"I'll make it up to you, I promise," Jack said, walking slowly again, not taking his eyes from the other man's. "Just drop the knife and let her go."

"I don't think I'll do that, Jack," Moe said sweetly. He fingered a strand of Elizabeth's hair, and Jack's chest tightened when he saw the panic on her face. "Kids just don't learn anything unless you teach them a good lesson. Don't you agree, *Jack?*"

"These folks have learned plenty, and they're ready to go home," Jack said in a low, hypnotic voice.

"*Five* of them *will* go home. And tell all their friends about their exciting camping trip," Moe said brightly. "One of them will stay behind in a pool of blood, to pay for their foolishness."

Jack stared back at Moe. Trying to negotiate on Elizabeth's behalf obviously wasn't working. He knew he had to come up with a better plan, and fast. "Hey, Moe, remember that guy in prison who told us about the gold in Death Valley?" Jack asked. He leaned casually against the cave wall.

"Yeah, what about him?" Moe asked suspiciously.

"Well, he told me this was only the beginning. He said there's plenty more, and we haven't even tapped the surface of it," Jack continued, making up his story as fast as he could.

"He did?" Moe said. He still sounded skeptical, but he definitely looked interested.

"He did. He told me the exact cave to go to, where there's five times more gold than this," Jack said in an excited tone. "So let's quit fooling around here, and go get more gold."

"As soon as I slit this young lady's throat, perhaps we can go sit someplace quiet and talk about it," Moe said graciously.

"No!" Todd yelled. He took a step forward and Bruce grabbed him.

"Todd, stay back," Elizabeth managed to say.

"Shut up," Moe hissed, and ran the smooth blade of the knife along Elizabeth's cheek. Elizabeth opened her mouth in a wide, soundless scream.

"No deal, Moe," Jack answered with a big smile. "Either you let her go, or you get no information—and no more gold."

Moe frowned. Then he shook his head and began to chuckle. "We've been through a lot together, haven't we buddy?" he said with a generous laugh.

"Sure have," Jack said.

"And we'll stick together and make each other rich, right?" Moe said warmly.

"To the end, pal," Jack said sincerely. Elizabeth's pleading eyes were the size of dinner plates. Jack stared into those frightened eyes with a bold look of reassurance. Yet he knew that Moe was capable of slicing her to ribbons at any moment.

"So what do you say?" Jack proposed, determined to give it one more try. "Put down the knife and let this pretty girl go back to her friends. Then we'll take off and get into some serious gold mining."

"No."

"Be reasonable," Jack said gently, staring with blazing intensity into Moe's hideously contorted face. Jack wondered if he'd seriously miscalculated just how much of a cold-blooded killer the man really was.

"You and I have had trouble seeing eye to eye on a few things, haven't we, my friend?" Moe said. "In fact, I think we've been heading for a showdown for a little while now."

"Or maybe we just need to talk, work it out," Jack said in a soothing voice, moving again toward Moe and Elizabeth. "We're friends, remember?"

Jack knew the situation had reached a point of no return. Only one of them would leave the cave alive. Jack was determined to get rid of Moe once and for all. He fixed his eyes on the bag of gold in Moe's hand, the same hand that was gripping Elizabeth. He knew what his next move would be.

Jessica gripped Ken's hand in the dim light of the dank cave and felt him grip back.

"This is my fault," Jessica whispered to Ken.

"You didn't set a bunch of convicts loose in the desert, Jess," Ken whispered back, wiping a tear from her cheek. He kissed her hair and cupped her face in his hand.

"Too bad your boyfriend didn't manage to steal my gun, huh? You won't get out of here alive," Larry suddenly hissed into Jessica's ear. He'd been standing there, hovering over Jessica for what seemed like years. She wished he'd just get lost.

"The day isn't over yet," Jessica whispered back.

"It may be over soon," Larry said. He pulled Jessica away from Ken, grabbing her chin in one hand and forcing her face up, so that she had no choice but to look at Elizabeth.

"She'll die quickly, don't worry," Larry continued. "Moe's an expert with knives. First he'll—"

"I don't need a technical play-by-play, thank you very much," Jessica interrupted. Larry sure seemed to be getting a kick out of this.

"But Moe is an artist when it comes to murder! Watch him and you'll see his genius," Larry whispered.

"So . . . what do you do in your free time, hang out at public executions?" Jessica asked, jerking her face out of Larry's grip. Ken quickly pulled her back into his arms.

"Don't touch her again," Ken said with quiet fury. He stroked Jessica's head.

"You haven't been very nice to me," Larry said, practically breathing down Jessica's neck. "That could be extremely unwise. Why don't you and I try to be friends?" Jessica felt Larry's eyes on her, while her heart froze at the tone of his threat.

157

Then she heard Elizabeth gasp for breath, as if she were drowning. Jessica's heart twisted. *How dare he hurt my twin sister!*

Jessica felt angry resolve rising from her toes, pushing away her fear. She didn't believe in dumb things like curses. Moe was an idiot not to have noticed Jessica lifting the gold from his pack. The least he could do was admit he was stupid and let them all go.

Jessica was sick of even thinking about gold. And she was sick of being terrorized by these two cruel convicts.

"I've got all the friends I need," Jessica said to Larry through clenched teeth. "So back off." Jessica could see Larry's stricken eyes in the half-light.

"You'll be sorry," Larry said, and moved back into the shadows along the cave wall.

"All you have to do is let Elizabeth go, and you'll be rich," Jessica heard Jack say.

"Why do I have this nagging feeling that I shouldn't trust you?" Moe replied.

Jessica had noticed that Jack was slowly inching toward Moe, ludicrously trying to talk him out of killing Elizabeth. Moe was obviously a maniac. *What does Jack think he's doing?* Jessica wondered.

Suddenly she realized exactly what he was doing. Jack knew perfectly well that martians would land in Death Valley before Moe would voluntarily release Elizabeth, even if he had three tons of gold waved in his face. Jack had some plan to move in on the man and take him by surprise.

If Jessica knew Jack's plan of action, she could help him. She felt certain, though, that whatever Jack wanted to do, she could help by distracting Moe's attention for a split second. Moe was about to cut Elizabeth's throat. Jessica had nothing to lose and no time to spare.

"Owww! I've got a terrible pain in my stomach!" she screamed. "It must be from the unpurified water!" She squeezed her arms around her middle and doubled over in fake agony.

"Jessica, what—" Ken said with alarm.

"Take her outside and shut her up!" Moe ordered Larry in a flustered voice, absently dropping his knife a few inches below Elizabeth's neck. From her bent-over position Jessica glanced up. For a single instant her eyes locked with Jack's in a moment of penetrating understanding.

Then, without warning, Jack kicked the bag of gold out of Moe's hand. Momentarily stunned, Moe loosened his hold on Elizabeth, and she bolted away from him into Todd's arms.

Jack lunged and grabbed Moe's wrist. Moe's hand sprang wide-open, and the knife clattered onto the rocky floor of the cave. Jack dived for the knife.

"It's either you or me!" he shouted. He slashed at Moe's leg with the razor-sharp blade but managed only to slice through the material of the blue jumpsuit. Enraged, Moe drew his gun.

"*You lose!*" the man shrieked. He pulled the trigger. The shot went straight through Jack's heart.

The force of the bullet sent Jack flying back against the cave wall. He closed his eyes and slid to the ground in a dark pool of blood.

"Jack!" Jessica screamed. Ken clutched her hand. Elizabeth buried her head in Todd's shoulder. Heather began to sob. Bruce held her close, with horror etched into his face.

"All right, who wants to be next?" Moe snarled.

"Boss, can I finish off the rest of them?" Larry asked hopefully.

"Of course you can," Moe said, patting Larry on the shoulder. "You've been patient and hardworking. You deserve some recreation."

"How about if I shoot them one by one while the others stand and watch?" Larry suggested. He was gazing directly at Jessica! She quickly turned away from his horrible stare—only to face Jack's lifeless body slumped on the cold desert ground. Her heart felt as if it had been dropped from a hundred-foot cliff to smash on the rocks below. And now they were left alone at the mercy of Larry and Moe! Ken's warm hands embraced her shoulders. But her body still shook with terrible shudders.

"You get rid of them any way you want," Moe concluded, picking up the sack of gold and placing it deep in his knapsack.

"I choose this one as the first to go," Larry said, grabbing Jessica by the arm. She gasped as he shoved her up against the mossy wall. Jessica saw Ken's frightened, pleading eyes, and she tried to communicate with him silently. *Please remember me.*

160

"No," Jessica whispered to Larry. She was shaking her head, refusing to believe that her life was about to end.

"Yes," Larry whispered back. He aimed his gun at Jessica's head and cocked the trigger.

Chapter 13

"Prepare to die, princess," Larry said. He brought the barrel of the gun to Jessica's temple.

Jessica took one last look into Ken's desperate eyes. She saw the outline of his face in the semidarkness. She wanted to hold the memory of his features forever and take it with her when she died. She shut her eyes as the cold metal of the gun pressed on her skin.

Jessica suddenly heard the sound of a plane overhead.

"What's that?" Heather asked.

"It's not a bunch of bats, that's for sure," Todd said. He put his arm around Elizabeth's waist and craned his neck to see the sky outside the cave.

"It can't be a regular commercial jetliner. It's flying way too low to the ground," Bruce observed.

"I'm going outside to check this out," Moe told Larry, as he put his hands over his ears to block out the roar of the engines.

"What do you want me to do while you're gone, boss?" Larry asked, still training his pistol on Jessica. Moe cast an exasperated look at the ceiling.

"Just when I was beginning to develop faith in your capacity for complex reasoning, you need me to spell it out for you," Moe said with a deep sigh. "When I come back, I don't want to see a single one of these troublemakers alive." Moe pointed his finger around the group in a slow circle as he spoke, finally stopping on Jessica. "Especially that one," he said in conclusion.

"She's got about twenty seconds left to live, boss," Larry agreed. Ken closed his eyes and raked his hands through his hair. *Jessica,* he mouthed to her.

"Oh, and *Larry,* just one other thing," Moe said, placing a hand on Larry's shoulder.

"Uh, yeah, boss?"

"If I come back and any of these nice young people are still breathing, do you know what's going to happen?" Moe asked. *What is this?* Jessica thought. *A study session for final exams?*

"I don't think so, boss," Larry said, looking puzzled.

"I'm going to kill *you,*" Moe said. Moe and Larry faced each silently as Larry's face clouded over.

"You wouldn't really do that," Larry said.

"Yes. I would," Moe said, and he walked quickly out of the cave. Jessica listened to the crunch of his boots as he left. Elizabeth had buried her face in Todd's shoulder.

Jessica didn't know what was worse, imminently

164

being shot by Larry, or having her eardrums burst from the noise of the aircraft. It sounded as if the plane were going to land right on the rock outcropping above the cave.

Land on the outcropping! SVSS had sent a rescue team to find them! Jessica suddenly realized. If only she could stall Larry—before time ran out. She eyed the gleam of the man's gun and took a deep swallow.

"Larry, they've come looking for us," Jessica said, looking directly into his eyes.

"What are you talking about?" Larry said suspiciously.

"I'm sure the mission of that plane flying overhead is to find us," Jessica said.

"You're sure about that, huh? Right, and I'm Genghis Khan," Larry said, with a look of cruel amusement.

"We're days overdue on our expected return from this camping trip," Jessica continued. "And they told us at our desert survival training seminar that they would send a small plane out to track down any campers who were late coming in."

"Then I guess they're out of luck. They won't find any live campers to take back, will they?" Larry said.

"When they find you with our dead bodies strewn all around, won't they take you straight back to prison and throw away the key?" Jessica asked sweetly.

"I'll be long gone, darlin'," Larry said with a cruel chuckle.

"Maybe the plane isn't looking for us at all, Larry," Jessica added, trying desperately to stop the trembling in her body. "Maybe it's looking for you."

"Don't try to play any games with me," Larry said angrily. But Jessica could see that his hand was starting to shake slightly.

"I'm not playing games. Moe's the one who walked off and left you here," Jessica said innocently. "Did you really think he'd hang around to see them catch you red-handed for a killer? Do you think he plans to go back to prison with you?"

Jessica could feel the tension coming from every other member of her group. They were all counting on her. Could she succeed in turning Larry against Moe? Jessica stifled the fear that was climbing up from the pit of her stomach.

"He's my partner," Larry said between clenched teeth. "He'll be right back. But you'll never know, because you'll be dead by then."

"Not much of a partner, if you ask me," Jessica said, mustering a casual shrug. "He said he'd kill you."

"I told you, he's a genius," Larry hissed, placing both shaking hands around his gun. Jessica took a deep, slow breath while clutching at the dirt on the cave wall behind her.

"He's a total maniac and you know it," Jessica finally said. "He'll kill you anyway, even if you finish us off before he gets back."

Jessica saw the pupils of Larry's eyes dilate for an instant. She was getting to him. The shaking in his hands began to spread to the rest of his body.

"Besides, Larry, I know you don't really want to kill me," Jessica said, gazing directly into the man's

166

hard eyes. "I meant what I said before. That there's a decent guy inside you somewhere."

Larry began shaking violently.

"I've got exactly six bullets, one for each of you," he said. His voice quavered.

"Please don't kill me, Larry," Jessica pleaded quietly, searching his face with her large blue eyes.

Without moving his eyes from Jessica's, Larry slowly lowered the gun. He stepped toward her and reached out with a rough hand. Jessica saw the confusion in his face as he caressed her hair and ran his fingers gently across her skin. She caught sight of Ken's perplexed, angry eyes. Larry leaned forward and kissed her lightly on the cheek. Then he leaned back and stepped away from her.

"All right. Get out of here, and make sure I never see you again," Larry whispered hoarsely through clenched teeth.

Larry aimed the gun straight up. He fired six shots at the ceiling of the cave, then dropped the gun onto the ground. He gazed at Jessica one last time. Then he ran out of the cave.

Ken rushed to Jessica and covered her face with kisses. He crushed her to him in a powerful embrace.

"I thought I'd lost you," he said, pressing his lips against hers.

The gravelly earth began to rumble. Dirt and stones fell in chunks from the cave ceiling.

"What's happening?" Heather shrieked.

"The gunshots have caused a cave-in!" Bruce said. "Let's get out of here!"

167

Jessica grabbed Ken's hand and turned to run from the cave. But before she had taken two steps, a huge block of hardened dirt tumbled onto the cave floor, blocking the entrance. There was no way out.

"I can't see a thing!" Todd called out, coughing.

Jessica felt soil and rocks tumbling down around her. She held her arms over her head and face for protection. She'd almost gotten used to the idea of being shot to death. *But being crushed in a cave-in? This is not how I want to go!*

The collapse slowed to a stop. Jessica felt the crush of dead silence. And there was no light at all.

"Is anyone else still alive?" she called out in a trembling voice.

"I'm afraid so," Bruce answered from somewhere.

"Yup," Ken said. He found Jessica in the dark and put his arms around her.

"At your service, ma'am," Todd said.

"If you call this alive," Elizabeth sighed.

"Nice job, Jessica," Heather said sarcastically. Then everyone fell silent again. Jessica breathed a deep sigh of relief.

"Well, I guess you're all wondering why I called you here," Jessica said. But absolutely nobody laughed. She had to admit she wasn't exactly in the mood for being the life of the party. She wondered vaguely if that plane really was looking for them. Not that it mattered anymore. The loosened dirt and rocks had sealed off the entrance to the cave.

Elizabeth felt her way to where the entrance had been. Her fingers touched cold rock.

"Somebody help me push the rocks away from the entrance," she called out.

"Feels like several big boulders are in our way," Todd said, putting his arm around Elizabeth. She felt the warmth of his breath but shuddered with cold fear.

"Well, let's get them *out* of our way," Bruce said impatiently.

Elizabeth pushed with all her might against the heavy, dirt-covered rocks. She heard the hard breathing and scuffling of the others as they forced their weight against the boulders.

"It's no use. They won't budge," Ken finally said.

"So now we get to die slowly of starvation or even suffocation, instead of getting finished off quickly," Heather said accusingly.

"Well, you're not dead yet—unfortunately," Jessica responded from the pitch-blackness.

"We probably will be within a few hours," Heather snapped.

"I'd say you should be getting down on your knees and groveling thanks to me right now," Jessica shot back.

Elizabeth took a shallow breath of the warm, dusty air and listened to the unbelievable bickering between Heather and Jessica. She couldn't see a thing in the total darkness. She leaned against the cave wall and closed her eyes in exhaustion.

Elizabeth could still feel the chilling metal of

Larry's blade on her throat, Jessica had just narrowly escaped being shot, and now they were all sealed in a cave that resembled a cellar with no doors or windows. Fighting among the group was definitely not what they needed.

Her stomach tightened. Was it possible that they might suffocate if they didn't find a way to get out of the cave?

"Stop arguing, you two. You're wasting air," Elizabeth said firmly.

"Yeah, Heather, you're using too much oxygen," Jessica said, which set off a fresh round of nastiness between the two.

Elizabeth sighed. She took a few small steps, being careful not to trip over anything in the dark, and ran smack into one of the guys.

"Is that you, Todd?" she asked, brushing her hand across the short, thick hair of the person in front of her.

"It's me, Bruce," came the reply. "But you don't have to stop running your fingers through my hair," he teased. Elizabeth quickly withdrew her hand and Bruce laughed gently. *Well, at least in complete darkness no one can see you blush,* Elizabeth thought.

"What do we do now?" Ken asked.

"Let's call everyone we know and have a wild party," Bruce suggested.

"You're a tremendous help in a crisis, Bruce," Todd said. Elizabeth felt Todd's hand find hers.

"Well, what do you want me to say? This is weird. It's like being at a seance," Bruce said.

170

"No, a seance would be better," Heather said. "At least then we'd have candles."

"I hate to admit this, but I unloaded my flashlight on the trail to make room in my pack for the gold," Todd said with a sigh.

"Same here," Ken said. Heather, Jessica, and Bruce had no flashlights either.

"We are totally sunk without any light," Jessica said gloomily.

"This is all your fault, Jessica," Heather started up again.

"*My* fault? It's my fault that you aren't poppy fertilizer right now," Jessica retorted.

Elizabeth rolled her eyes as she dug into her pack. She quickly found what she was looking for and stood up. She flicked the switch on her flashlight.

"I said knock it off," Elizabeth commanded, shining the beam of light right into Jessica's eyes, then Heather's.

"Way to go, Elizabeth," Bruce said.

"Well, somewhere along the trail some happy ravens are enjoying the trail mix I stupidly tossed aside to make room in my own pack for the gold," Elizabeth admitted. "But I did manage to hang on to my flashlight."

Elizabeth tracked the flashlight slowly across the cave, lighting up Bruce, Ken, Todd, Heather, and Jessica like lanterns. Everyone's face was smudged with dirt and mud.

"We all look like coal miners," Elizabeth said.

"My hair is never going to recover," Heather

complained, picking up a long strand of matted blonde hair.

"You'll probably have to shave your head," Jessica offered cheerfully.

"I wouldn't talk," Heather snapped back. "You'll have to buy stock in a shampoo company if you ever expect to get the mud out of your—"

But Heather stopped speaking in midsentence as Elizabeth's flashlight illuminated an unmoving, blood-stained figure. It was Jack, lying dead on the cave floor. No one spoke for a long moment.

"We've got to bury him," Todd finally said.

"We can use pans and cups for shovels," Elizabeth said, feeling the steady beat of her heart.

"We're all incredibly lucky to be alive," Ken said hoarsely. "I don't know how we're going to survive now. But we have to hand it to Jess that we even have the option to try." Ken reached for Jessica's hand. Elizabeth watched the shadows play across his face in the dim light.

Jessica's gaze was fixed on Jack. Heather was also staring silently at Jack's limp, dead body.

"I guess I do owe you some thanks, Jessica," Heather mumbled. "Can't argue with the fact that we're not dead yet."

Elizabeth shined the yellow beam of the flashlight directly onto Heather's face. She was surprised by what she saw. Heather was smiling weakly at Jessica, without a trace of malice or superiority.

"Nope, not dead yet," Jessica agreed. She offered Heather a slight smile in return.

"Let's take care of Jack," Elizabeth said soberly. "Then we'll search for a way out of here."

"I can't believe he's dead," Elizabeth said, looking at Jack's finished grave site. Even though the cave was warm and wet, she felt numb, as if she were standing up to her neck in a solid block of ice. Todd sat down on the ground and pulled Elizabeth down next to him. Then Ken, Heather, and Bruce sat cross-legged next to them in a circle around the grave.

"Jess, are you going to come sit with us for a minute?" Elizabeth asked, propping up the flashlight inside the circle. She turned around and caught sight of Jessica slumped against the cave wall, her legs tucked up close to her body.

"No, I can't stand hanging around dead bodies," Jessica responded, her voice completely flat.

"Gee, thanks," Bruce called over his shoulder.

In the semidarkness Elizabeth could see a single tear sliding down Jessica's face.

Elizabeth turned back to the grave and stared at the mound of sand, gravel, and dirt under which Jack was now buried.

"He was trying to help me," Elizabeth said quietly. "And he lost his own life."

"Liz, do you think that story he told Moe about another cave full of gold was true?" Todd asked.

"No, I don't think so," Elizabeth said, shaking her head slowly. "I think he made it up to distract him until he could get the knife away." Everyone fell silent. Elizabeth felt a spontaneous shudder pass

173

through her body at the mere thought of Moe's sharp knife.

But she was alive, whereas all of Jack's dreams about going back to school and making a fresh start were dust.

"His girlfriend back home is really going to miss him," Todd said.

Elizabeth put her arms around Todd. She tilted her face to him, and his lips touched hers. If she survived to see one more night sky, or smell a rose, or hear music, she would never take the ordinary, precious things and people of her life for granted again.

"You guys, I'm starting to feel really tired," Heather said all of a sudden.

"I know. It's hot in here," Ken said.

"Maybe we should all rest for a while before trying to blast our way out of here," Bruce yawned. "It's been kind of a long day."

"No!" Elizabeth said instinctively. "We may be starting to run out of air. We can't fall asleep."

"We could lose consciousness and not wake up," Todd said, finishing Elizabeth's thought. Todd stood quickly and brushed himself off. "There has got to be a way out."

"Hey, Elizabeth, shine the flashlight over here," Jessica said from the darkness. Jessica had probably got bored sitting off by herself and started wandering around the cave, exploring. Elizabeth sent the beam over in the direction of Jessica's voice.

"Look at that!" Bruce said, whistling.

"The cave goes deeper into the rock wall," Todd observed with wonder.

Elizabeth stared in amazement at the passageway. *Where does it lead?* she wondered. *What if it only takes us deeper under the desert until we lose our way for good?* "Our only choice is to see where Jessica's surprise route will take us," Elizabeth said. Jessica tossed her a smug look. Elizabeth rolled her eyes at her sister and crossed her fingers. *Yes, Jessica, you may have saved the day again. We hope.*

"This could be tricky, walking through a pitch-black cave with only the light of a single flashlight," Ken said, peering into the passageway.

"I was thinking the same thing," Elizabeth agreed. "We may need to call on some of our basic skills from the training seminar."

"Like what? It's not like there's a lot of wide-open space for someone to meander off into and get lost," Jessica pointed out.

"That actually might not be true," Ken said. "I remember them saying at SVSS that there are often multiple forks in the passages in these caves. If you take a wrong turn in the dark, we may never see you again."

"Right, that's why we need to reestablish our buddy system," Elizabeth said. "And for extra safety it's important that we stay with our original partners."

Jessica could have screamed. Stuck again with Todd. And Heather would be paired with Ken—in almost total darkness. *I know you're out there smirking in the dark, Mallone,* Jessica thought irritably.

It was totally unfair. Jessica had come inches from being shot and losing Ken forever. And despite her ingenuity in scouting out the passageway, there was still no guarantee that she would make it out of the cave alive. After saving everyone else from Larry and Moe, she deserved to spend what could be her last moments on earth feeling the reassuring touch of Ken's hand in hers.

Jessica opened her mouth to protest, but Elizabeth and Bruce had already stepped into the passage together, followed by Ken and Heather.

"After you, Jess," Todd said cheerfully.

"Please, no Ranger Rick enthusiasm. I'm not in the mood," Jessica said dryly. She followed Heather into the narrow tunnel.

Jessica figured there wasn't enough oxygen for Todd to talk much. That was the one saving grace of this cramped, hot trek—which could lead to a molten-lava pit in the center of the earth as easily as it could lead outside.

After a few minutes Jessica noticed with annoyance that she wasn't marching through hard-packed sandy earth anymore. The ground had turned to mud.

"Hey, my feet are getting wet," Jessica said.

"Mine are, too," Todd said in a puzzled tone. "It looks like a small stream of water is running through this passageway."

"At least no one will get lost," Elizabeth called from the front of the line. "As long as our feet are wet, we'll know we're on the right track."

Everyone laughed. Everyone except Ken, Jessica noticed.

"I don't see what's so funny," Ken said with an edge in his voice.

What's his problem? Jessica wondered. *Maybe I'm glad we're not walking together, if Ken is this grouchy.* So what if there was some water in the cave? It wasn't the worst thing in the world.

Jessica continued to trudge sulkily alongside Todd for what seemed like years. She distracted herself from the tedium of the hike with visions of a siesta by the Wakefields' swimming pool under a blue sky.

Jessica snapped awake from her daydream as she realized she was up to her ankles in water.

"What's going on? I feel like I'm walking through a swamp," Heather complained. "My shoes will be ruined."

"This is what I was afraid of," Ken murmured.

"What, that Heather's nice cheerleading shoes wouldn't survive the camping trip?" Bruce asked.

"Bruce, don't you see what Ken's getting at?" Jessica asked with alarm. "The water's already up to the middle of my calf."

"It's the flood," Ken said, confirming Jessica's worst fear. "It's found its way inside the cave. The water level is rising higher by the second."

Jessica realized with horror why Ken hadn't

laughed at Elizabeth's joke. She rushed over to him and grabbed his arm.

"We've got to find the end of this passageway," Ken said urgently, stroking Jessica's hair. "If we don't get out of here soon, we'll drown."

Chapter 14

"Step up the pace!" Ken yelled, sloshing through the water as it rapidly filled the cave.

"Ouch, Jessica! You stepped on my foot," Todd yowled.

"Well, I'm sorry," Jessica snapped. "It's a little dark in here, if you hadn't noticed."

Elizabeth slogged on through the sea of floating brush, wading up to her knees. She was trying hard to remember that the group had endured every danger possible during the course of this desert nightmare but still managed to come through each crisis and work together. Now chaos threatened to break out again and destroy any chance for survival.

"Out of my way!"

"Get your hair out of my face!"

"We're going to die in here!"

Elizabeth couldn't stand it. Everyone was yelling at once as they all scrambled to move quickly through the cave and escape the treacherous floodwaters. The buddy system was in shambles. They'd be lucky if no one fell and got trampled in the dark water.

"My ankle!" Heather cried.

"Heather, I'll buy you a new one when we get home if you'll just shut up and keep moving," Jessica said through clenched teeth.

"But I can't go that fast!" she protested. "And everyone keeps crashing into me."

"Then step aside and let the able-bodied go first. Follow behind us," Jessica said with exasperation.

"No, I don't want to go last! What if you guys get way ahead and I'm left alone to drown?" Heather whimpered.

"Everyone settle down. We'll never get any-where if we keep acting like bumper cars," Elizabeth said, pushing through the rising water. She kept her flashlight trained straight ahead. *Just keep going forward, keep following the light!* she told herself.

"Too bad I forgot my fly-fishing outfit. The water is up to my thighs," Jessica said, taking big, splashing steps.

Heather suddenly screamed, splashing wildly. Elizabeth turned and frantically flashed the thin beam of light onto Heather's face, which was bobbing just above the water.

"Somebody help Heather get up! We don't have time to waste!" Elizabeth yelled, losing her nerve.

"Heather, *please*," Bruce begged, hoisting her up. "What about all the Olympic gymnasts who bust their ankles in the middle of their floor routines and keep going to the end?"

"I'm a cheerleader. I'm not an Olympic gymnast," Heather sobbed. "And I can't walk!"

"Then start swimming!" Todd yelled.

The water was licking at Elizabeth's chest and still rising. At least when she'd been hanging off the edge of a cliff, she knew that she'd be able to keep breathing all the way down. Now she might be enjoying the last gasps of air she'd ever take.

"If we swim fast enough, maybe we'll find a way out," Ken sputtered.

Elizabeth struggled to swim. Her backpack kept sliding off, and she kept trying to push the straps back onto her shoulders while holding on to the flashlight at the same time. She coughed and choked as water splashed into her mouth. Finally she let the pack slide off her shoulders to sink in the murky water.

"I knew I should have completed my senior life-saving course," Jessica gasped.

"Maybe if we all scream, someone will hear us," Heather said.

"We're at the absolute center of the earth. No one can hear us," Jessica responded.

"Elizabeth!" Todd hollered. "Let me take the flashlight—you need both hands to stay afloat."

Todd swam past Ken, Bruce, and Heather and reached Elizabeth's side as she splashed in the rising waters.

"I can handle it," Elizabeth gasped. "Don't

worry about me. Just keep swimming!"

"No! I won't let you take care of everyone else," Todd said. "Give me the flashlight." He grabbed the flashlight and tried to pull it out of Elizabeth's grasp. Loose gravel rained down on her from the walls of the cave. She felt something inside her snap.

"Todd, leave it!" she yelled. But Todd jerked the flashlight out of her hand and fell back into the water. Bruce came sailing into Todd, knocking the flashlight right out of his hand. It flew into the water and sank straight to the bottom. The cave plunged into total darkness.

"I can't see a thing!" Heather screamed in horror.

Elizabeth felt the water rise to her shoulders and then to her neck.

"It's almost to the top of the cave," Jessica said in terror as she coughed and splashed.

"Elizabeth, I'm sorry," Todd said through the pitch-blackness.

"Sorry for what?" Elizabeth asked.

"I'm sorry I have to die in the dark without being able to see you once more," he answered.

"Somebody somewhere please help us!" Heather shrieked at the top of her lungs.

Just then Elizabeth felt the water level drop from her mouth to her neck.

Then the water receded to her shoulders.

"The flood level is falling," Ken said in amazement.

"The rain must have stopped!" Bruce shouted.

Elizabeth felt her feet touch the cave floor again.

182

The floodwater was draining away, just as fast as it had come. *This desert is so strange!* Her heart was pounding as she drew a deep, shaky breath.

In the blackness Elizabeth felt Todd touch her cold cheek and warmly kiss her.

"We're going to make it," he whispered.

The water fell to Elizabeth's chest. Her shoulders felt cold as they became exposed to the air. She touched the wet walls of the cave with her hands. *We're alive and breathing. But where are we?* she asked herself.

"We're safe," Heather said, exhaling. She sat right down in the last foot of water. Bruce sat in the water next to her and slumped against the wall.

"This is absolutely the last time I go camping in the desert without bringing my scuba equipment," Bruce said, his chest heaving.

"Diving. That makes me think of the beach," Todd said, closing his eyes and sighing deeply. He opened one eye. "I'll race you into the ocean as soon as we get back to Sweet Valley."

"Deal," Bruce said.

"With a quick stop at Dairi Burger before we dash into the sea," Heather added in a tired voice.

"Good idea," Todd laughed.

Jessica didn't quite feel like joining the celebration banter. Instead she walked uneasily around in the water, trying to feel her way in the dark.

"Ken, is that you?" she said, touching a strong shoulder.

"It's me," he said, pulling her into his arms. He found her lips and she melted into his kiss. She stepped closer to him and felt something smooth and round beneath her foot.

"I think I found the flashlight," Jessica whispered to Ken.

She quickly bent down and ran her hands through the shallow water at her feet. Her fingers touched the metallic casing of the flashlight, and she picked it up. It had turned off when it hit the rocky ground. Jessica pressed the switch and shone the beam on Ken's chest. Shadows flew across his strong face.

"It's nice to see you again," Jessica said quietly. "I've missed you." Ken smiled and pressed his warm hand to her cheek.

Then Jessica moved the flashlight beam onto the walls and ceiling of the cave.

"If you see any spiderwebs, let me know and I'll call the maid," Bruce joked.

"You guys, I never want to be the one to spoil a great party, but I have one slightly unpleasant question to ask," Jessica said.

"What's that?" Todd asked, resting his feet on a rock and locking his hands behind his head.

"We may be able to put away the snorkeling equipment, but how are we going to get out of here?" Jessica asked. No one moved or spoke for about five seconds.

"Great," Ken groaned in frustration. "We've been saved, but we're still who knows where, who knows how far underground."

"And we have no food," Bruce said.

"And, ironically, no water to drink," Elizabeth added. Everyone fell silent again.

"Thank you. I think that answers my question," Jessica said. "We have no idea what to do next."

"This is so ridiculous!" Ken exclaimed, pacing in the muddy water. "How can we escape the guns and knives of a couple of desperate men, only to die trapped in a stupid cave? It doesn't make sense!"

"Ken, calm down," Jessica said, placing a hand on his shoulder.

"No! I don't want to calm down," Ken said. "There's no way out!"

Jessica bit her lip as Ken suddenly punched the wall in frustration.

"Ken, you're losing it!" Jessica cried, horrified. "You can't go crazy like this. If we all start panicking, we'll never get home."

"We'll never get home as it is!" Ken said angrily. "So why should I be deprived of the final pleasure of going totally crazy?"

Ken drew back his arm and released one more powerful punch straight into the cave wall. Jessica felt as if she were watching him moving in slow motion.

But as Ken's fist impacted with the hard soil, the wall suddenly gave way in big chunks and crumbled onto the ground. Jessica stared at the gaping hole that was left in the rock face.

"Either you've been lifting six-ton barbells in your free time, or this wall isn't made of solid rock," Jessica observed with amazement.

"It's just shale!" Elizabeth exclaimed. "Ken, remember when we were climbing that high trail? I thought I was standing on solid granite, but then it crumbled under me. This rock is really shale!"

"We can dig our way out!" Jessica said excitedly.

"But we don't know how far down we are. What if the whole ceiling caves in?" Bruce argued.

"I don't see that we have much choice," Elizabeth pointed out.

"What's the matter, Bruce, have you suddenly got afraid to take a few risks?" Jessica teased, flashing a smile.

"I'd say this whole trip has turned out to be one huge, scary unknown," Todd said, giving Elizabeth's arm a squeeze.

"So let's go for it," Elizabeth said.

"You Wakefields can actually sound sensible when you're forced to," Bruce conceded.

"I'll hold the flashlight," Heather volunteered, curling a lock of stringy hair around her finger.

"No way, Mallone. You'll have to put your nail file and polish up for sale after this," Jessica said. "Start digging."

Everyone began punching and pounding on the cave wall, as it easily fell apart under their hands. Jessica clawed with one hand and held the light with the other. She gave the wall a kick with her steel-toed boot, and a tremendous sheet of rock broke free and fell into rubble at her feet.

"Somebody pinch me. Am I dreaming, or am I really punching out a rock wall hundreds of feet below the earth's crust?" Bruce said.

"Just be careful where you're hacking," Todd said as he worked. "You wouldn't want to be responsible for jarring a fault line and setting off a major earthquake."

"I'll keep it in mind," Bruce answered.

"I can't do this anymore," Elizabeth finally said, falling back exhausted.

"Don't quit yet, Liz. Look!" Jessica called from a few feet away. "Don't you see it?"

"See what? I don't see anything," Elizabeth said, catching her breath.

Jessica walked over to Elizabeth and pulled her to her feet. "Come on, I've got a surprise for you," Jessica said.

"I love surprises," Elizabeth responded limply.

Jessica put her hands on her sister's shoulders and steered her toward the fist-sized hole in the shale wall.

"Look through here," Jessica said quietly.

Elizabeth fell onto her knees and looked through the hole. "Stars! I saw stars!" Elizabeth screamed. She leaped to her feet and threw her arms around Jessica.

Everyone gasped.

With a whoop of glee the group resumed pounding and clawing the wall with renewed vigor. The last layer crumbled, and cool night air filled the cave.

"Feel the breeze," Elizabeth whispered to Todd.

"Where are we, anyway? Did we dig to China?"

Bruce griped. They hauled themselves through the opening, one by one.

Jessica gazed up at the Big Dipper. "Hey!" she said happily. She began howling with laughter. The others turned to look in the direction of her gaze.

"I don't believe it, I thought we had two days of hiking left," Todd said, his jaw dropping.

"I guess the cave turned out to be a shortcut," Heather said with awe.

"Who cares? We're fifty yards from the parking lot of the Desert Oasis 7-Eleven!" Bruce shouted.

Chapter 15

"I'd say you're all looking pretty healthy," the SVSS staff doctor said, removing her stethoscope from Bruce's chest.

Kay Jansen leaned into the clinic entrance. "Now that you've all been checked out, come on into my office," she said warmly.

Elizabeth flopped into a chair near Kay's desk. Even though it had been three days since their return to civilization, she still couldn't quite believe she was back at the Sweet Valley Survival headquarters. But here she was—sitting in Kay's comfortable office, in fresh jeans and a T-shirt, her hair clean and silky.

"The managers at the 7-Eleven were really nice to us," Todd said. The owners had been warned that six lost campers might come staggering in at any time.

"When our mud-caked group dragged into the store, the clerks knew right away who we were," Heather said.

"We must have looked like *Night of the Living Dead*," Bruce added.

"No, only you, Bruce. The rest of us looked great," Jessica said, and everyone laughed easily.

"I'm getting the impression that you all got to know each other better out in the desert," Brad Mainzer observed.

"We certainly did," Elizabeth confirmed. "And by the way, thanks for coming all the way out to Desert Oasis to get us, Brad."

While one of the 7-Eleven managers had given the group free fruit juice, the other had called SVSS. Brad had driven out in the SVSS minivan to pick them up himself.

Kay put some folders away in her filing cabinet and closed the metal drawer. Then she sat down behind her desk. She opened a spiral notebook, uncapped a pen, and gave everyone a big smile.

"OK, we want to hear everything," Kay said.

"You guys looked like you'd been through quite an ordeal when I picked you up," Brad said. "Who wants to go first?"

"It's hard to know where to begin," Elizabeth said, rubbing her hands nervously on her wooden folding chair. She wasn't sure she even wanted to tell Kay and Brad that the group had gone off the trail and abandoned most of their supplies, all because of a greedy attempt to go after a few sacks of gold.

"Why don't you start at the beginning?" Kay suggested. Elizabeth cleared her throat.

"It all started when we found the gold," Jessica said brightly.

"What gold?" Kay said with a blank stare. Elizabeth closed her eyes. *Here it comes.*

But then Elizabeth realized that spilling the whole truth was the right thing to do. Both the gold and the diary were historically significant. Elizabeth had hoped to write an article about them. *Maybe I still can!* she suddenly realized.

"We found sacks of gold in the mine shafts," Elizabeth finally explained.

"I distinctly remember warning you not to go into the mine shafts," Brad said, raising an eyebrow.

"I know," Elizabeth admitted sheepishly. "But we found a diary from 1849, written by a traveler who came through Death Valley in a wagon train," Elizabeth explained.

"Well, I've done a lot of historic reading about the California deserts," Brad said. "And there hasn't been gold in those mine shafts for a hundred years."

"But—" Elizabeth stammered. How could that be?

"We saw it with our own eyes," Ken said.

"Hmmmm," Kay said skeptically.

"You should check your sources," Jessica said. She reached into her pocket and proudly pulled out a single gold nugget, to the surprise of the entire group. "I managed to save just one," Jessica said, shrugging at Elizabeth. "I figured it's at least worth an Italian bathing suit at Lisette's."

Brad took the nugget and turned it over in his palm. Elizabeth held her breath and glanced over at

191

Jessica, who was on the edge of her seat.

"Well, young lady, you should check your minerals," Brad finally said. Laughing, he handed the nugget back to Jessica. "That's nothing but ordinary pyrite."

"What's pyrite?" Jessica asked.

"Fool's gold," Brad answered, tapping his pen on his notebook.

Jessica's jaw dropped so far, it almost hit the floor. Elizabeth felt her heart skip a full beat.

"But what . . . what about the diary?" Elizabeth stammered.

"Well, if you have it, let's take a look," Kay said.

"I saved it in a plastic bag in my pack and brought it with me," Elizabeth said, handing the diary over to Brad.

"Certainly looks authentic," Brad said, flipping through the pages. "It's an excellent reproduction. But I can tell from the paper and the leather binding that it was made in the last few years."

"It was probably created by a theater group trying to reenact the feel of the gold rush for a stage production," Kay suggested.

"They probably planted the skeletons, too," Jessica said, sinking in her chair.

Elizabeth wished she could crawl under a stage set herself at that very moment. She cast a dazed look at her stunned sister.

"There's just one other thing we need to discuss," Brad said.

"What's that?" Elizabeth asked warily.

"A plane we sent to rescue your group picked up a pair of escaped convicts instead and brought them safely back to prison," Brad explained. He put down his pen and folded his hands on his desk.

"Really?" Jessica said with wide eyes. She gaped at Heather and Ken, who exchanged looks with Todd and Bruce.

"But the prisoners kept mumbling that if only a certain group of kids hadn't got in their way, they'd be across the border with sacks of gold by now," Kay added, raising both eyebrows.

"And when the prison directors asked if they knew the names of those kids, they said . . . Elizabeth and Jessica," Brad said, leaning forward in his chair. "I think the state authorities would like to see all of you and get the real story."

"Save me a seat somewhere," Elizabeth said to Bruce as she looked around the crowded lunchroom at Sweet Valley High. It was their first day back at school since the camping trip.

"We're all going to sit together at the table by the window," Bruce told her, loading extra brownies and an apple onto his tray.

"If it isn't Lewis and Clark," Winston Egbert said, suddenly appearing with Maria Santelli.

"I believe Lewis and Clark explored the Oregon wilderness," Elizabeth corrected him as she selected a chef's salad. "The California desert is a little different."

"Hey, I dressed in your honor today," Winston

chirped, undaunted. "Since I knew you were just back from Death Valley."

"A skull-and-crossbones T-shirt. Very nice, Winston," Elizabeth said with a nod of approval.

"Can we come sit with you? We want to hear all about your trip," Maria said.

"Sure," Elizabeth said. "Follow me."

A few minutes later Heather, Ken, and Todd all set their trays down at the window table.

"Nice Ace bandage, Heather," Winston observed. "What happened? Did you trip over a roadrunner?"

"No, I twisted my ankle running from a ruthless escaped convict," Heather answered coolly.

"Ha ha, very funny. It's all right, girls are always making fun of me," Winston said in a mock tone of hurt.

Just then Enid Rollins came rushing into the lunchroom clutching a newspaper. She waved to Elizabeth and ran through the lunch crowd over to the window table.

"Have you seen the front page of today's paper?" Enid asked excitedly. "You guys are heroes! Listen to this headline: 'Sweet Valley High School Leaders Bust Notorious Criminals'!"

Jessica sashayed into the cafeteria with Lila Fowler. "The sunsets were gorgeous, we ate gourmet food every night, and swam in the desert springs every day," Jessica was saying to Lila as they approached the table. Elizabeth rolled her eyes. Naturally, her sister was going to make this trip sound like a week on the French Riviera.

"Jessica, can we have your autograph?" Maria called.

"Of course. Do you have a pen with purple ink? Purple *is* my favorite color," Jessica said breezily, scanning the top story. "Actually, it was nothing at all." She set down the newspaper and flopped into a chair next to Elizabeth.

"That's right, we finished off those convicts the first afternoon and spent the rest of the trip sunbathing," Heather said, spooning strawberry yogurt into a bowl.

"Exactly," Jessica said. She exchanged a knowing smile with Heather.

"I only wish Jack was with us," Elizabeth said quietly.

"Same here," Jessica whispered, looking down at the table.

"The whole thing sounds charming—if you like to go camping," Lila declared, tossing her luxurious brown hair. "Personally, I couldn't stand carrying those heavy packs and having to go for days without a hot bath."

"I'll tell you what *I've* gone for days without," Jessica said with a sparkle in her eyes. "Shopping."

"This afternoon—you and me at the mall," Lila said urgently.

"I can't wait."

"But the first stop has to be at the jewelry store," Lila said, grabbing the sleeve of Jessica's lavender T-shirt. "Yesterday I saw a pair of gold earrings and a gold necklace that were *to die for*. I've got to have them. I absolutely love gold."

Elizabeth shot Bruce an amused look. She watched him glance at Todd and Ken, who smiled at Heather. They all pushed back their chairs and stood up from the table.

"You done with that math assignment?"

"Nope, have to hit the books before class."

"Sorry to eat and run."

"Catch you guys later."

They all grabbed their trays and strode off.

"What's eating them?" Elizabeth heard Lila say as she glanced back over her shoulder.

"Beats me," Jessica said with a shrug, winking at Elizabeth. "You know, though, Li, I've always preferred *silver* jewelry myself."

Bantam Books in the Sweet Valley High series
Ask your bookseller for the books you have missed

SIGN UP FOR THE SWEET VALLEY HIGH® FAN CLUB!

Hey, girls! Get all the gossip on Sweet Valley High's® most popular teenagers when you join our fantastic Fan Club! As a member, you'll get all of this really cool stuff:

- Membership Card with your own personal Fan Club ID number
- A Sweet Valley High® Secret Treasure Box
- Sweet Valley High® Stationery
- Official Fan Club Pencil (for secret note writing!)
- Three Bookmarks
- A "Members Only" Door Hanger
- Two Skeins of J. & P. Coats® Embroidery Floss with flower barrette instruction leaflet
- Two editions of *The Oracle* newsletter
- Plus exclusive Sweet Valley High® product offers, special savings, contests, and much more!

Be the first to find out what Jessica & Elizabeth Wakefield are up to by joining the Sweet Valley High® Fan Club for the one-year membership fee of only $6.25 each for U.S. residents, $8.25 for Canadian residents (U.S. currency). Includes shipping & handling.

Send a check or money order (do not send cash) made payable to "Sweet Valley High® Fan Club" along with this form to:

SWEET VALLEY HIGH® FAN CLUB, BOX 3919-B, SCHAUMBURG, IL 60168-3919

NAME _____
(Please print clearly)

ADDRESS _____

CITY _____ STATE _____ ZIP _____
(Required)

AGE _____ BIRTHDAY _____ / _____ / _____

It's Your
First Love. . .
Yours *and* His.

Love Stories

Nobody Forgets
Their First Love!

Now there's a romance series that gets to the heart of *everyone's* feelings about falling in love. *Love Stories* reveals how boys feel about being in love, too! In every story, a boy and girl experience the real-life ups and downs of being a couple, and share in the thrills, joys, and sorrows of first love.

Life after high school gets even *Sweeter!*

Jessica and Elizabeth are now freshmen at Sweet Valley University, where the motto is: Welcome to college — welcome to freedom!

Don't miss any of the books in this fabulous new series.

♥ College Girls #1	0-553-56308-4	$3.50/$4.50 Can.
♥ Love, Lies and Jessica Wakefield #2	0-553-56306-8	$3.50/$4.50 Can.
♥ What Your Parents Don't Know #3	0-553-56307-6	$3.50/$4.50 Can.
♥ Anything for Love #4	0-553-56311-4	$3.50/$4.50 Can.
♥ A Married Woman #5	0-553-56309-2	$3.50/$4.50 Can.
♥ The Love of Her Life #6	0-553-56310-6	$3.50/$4.50 Can.

Bantam Doubleday Dell
Books for Young Readers

Bantam Doubleday Dell
Dept. SVU 12
2451 South Wolf Road
Des Plaines, IL 60018

Please send the items I have checked above. I am enclosing $_____ (please add $2.50 to cover postage and handling). Send check or money order, no cash or C.O.D.s please.

_____
Name

_____
Address

_____
City   State   Zip

Please allow four to six weeks for delivery.
Prices and availability subject to change without notice.   SVU 12 4/94